HECK'S STAND

HECK & HOPE, BOOK 5

JOHN DEACON

Want to know when my next book is released? SIGN UP HERE.

❀ Created with Vellum

PROLOGUE

Heck's Stand is book five in the *Heck & Hope* series. I recommend reading the books in order, as they tell a continuing story. If you would like a refresher, here's the story so far, along with a list of characters.

Heck's Journey (Heck & Hope #1)

Orphaned at fourteen, Hector "Heck" Martin heads west, determined to see the far country and make a man of himself.

Along the way, he falls in love with bold and beautiful Hope Mullen. But Heck is too young and poor to marry, so he heads west again.

During a three-year journey, Heck crosses thousands of miles, becomes a bareknuckle boxer, a mountain man, and an

Indian fighter, and meets the likes of Kit Carson and Jim Bridger as he explores the gorgeous and deadly frontier.

Then, stopping by Fort Bent, he receives a letter that changes everything. Hope's family is daring the Oregon Trail.

Heck sets out to intercept and help them. Near the Oregon Trail in Wyoming, he throws in with another, younger orphan, Seeker, who becomes like a little brother to him.

Meanwhile, the Mullens face serious troubles—both outside and within the wagon train. When bandits attack, Mr. Mullen is badly injured, and the family loses its wagon and all their possessions. They are forced to live off the charity of the despicable Basil Paisley, a wealthy and cruel young man who wants to possess Hope.

Reunited with the Mullens, Heck saves them, kills Paisley and his thugs, and proposes to Hope, who happily accepts.

HECK'S VALLEY (HECK & HOPE #2)

AS A MOUNTAIN MAN AND CAVALRY SCOUT, HECK MARTIN handled every challenge on the Western frontier.

Now, however, he must care not only for himself but also his beloved Hope, her family, and his adopted brother, Seeker, in a remote wilderness populated by hostile Indians, bandits, and predators.

Most men would crumble under these circumstances, but Heck has enough love and courage to forge a new destiny in this mighty land. Filled with tough optimism and pioneering spirit, he vows to master the wilderness.

There is much to do.

Timber to cut. Cabins to build. Game to hunt. Land to plow and plant. A claim to stake. Caves to explore. A trading post to build. And hopefully, a happy wedding to share with the young woman he loves.

But Indians are moving through the land, and a gigantic grizzly is on the prowl. Meanwhile, 1850 brings record numbers of emigrants across the Oregon Trail. Not all are prepared, and as travel season comes to an end, a group of straggling emigrants limps into the valley, seeking sanctuary.

Heck and Hope agree to help, but not everyone should be trusted.

Most of the newcomers a good people. They bring important skills and work hard, helping mightily in the construction of the fort and the building of new roads.

Doctor Michael Skiff, who is also a pastor, marries Heck and Hope.

But newcomer Dave Chapman is secretly one of the bandits who attacked the Mullens' train and later got mostly wiped out by Heck and Seeker. He acts the part of a pleasant emigrant, but he really wants to kill Heck and steal away Hope and Amelia.

When Heck battles a giant grizzly bear, Dave shoots him in the back. Always tough, Heck barely manages to finish the bear and kill the backshooting bandit as well.

During Heck's long recovery, he comes to rely on his friends and family, who keep things moving. Eventually, he is able to return to the mysterious cave complex, where, in the final chapter, he discovers a massive nugget of gold.

· · ·

HECK'S GOLD (HECK & HOPE #3)

AFTER COMPLETING THEIR FORT, THE RESIDENTS OF HECK'S Valley brace for winter. Many speak of spring—and the possibility of staying here and working together to build a town in this breathtaking wilderness.

Heck and Hope don't know what the future holds, but so long as they are together, they face it with confidence.

But life on the frontier is never easy.

They have to guard their stock, keep the peace, and prepare defenses for spring, when the Sioux warriors who killed Seeker's parents will again come raiding.

When word of Heck's massive golden nugget leaks, there is trouble among the emigrants, but Heck handles it. He is determined to sit on the nugget indefinitely, as they don't need the money it represents.

After a brutal winter, most of the emigrants decide to stay. Working together, they create their town, which they dub Hope City.

With spring come raiders from the Bone Canyon Sioux. Seeker avenges his parents as the citizens of Hope City, with the help of Seeker's uncle, Black Cloud, ambush the raiders, wiping out all but one, a tough young brave named Little Bull, who rides back to his tribe carrying Heck's warning.

Jim Bridger shows up, bearing supplies and bad news. The price of the valley has gone up.

Accompanied by Bridger, Two Bits, and assayer Sam Collins, Heck travels to San Francisco and sell the nugget. Here, he gets involved with rough characters, including gang boss Bill

Getty and the new bareknuckle boxing champion of the West, Big Jess Heller.

Dodging Getty, Heck wagers everything on a fight against Heller. Beating the giant and reclaiming his old boxing title, Heck is suddenly flush with cash. He trades the nugget with Cattleman *Don* Vasquez for a herd of longhorn cattle, thereby making a mortal enemy in the nugget's would-be buyer, the richest man in California, gold baron Percival Dumay, who vows to get even with Heck.

On the trip home, Heck is attacked by Getty and his man but kills them easily.

Returning to the valley, he is overjoyed to be reunited with Hope—and to meet his newborn son, Hector Martin III, known as "Tor."

HECK'S GAMBLE (HECK & HOPE #4)

HECK MARTIN BATTLED INDIANS, BANDITS, AND GRIZZLY BEARS to make his valley the gem of the frontier. He overcame big obstacles to buy the land, build a town, and bring in a herd of longhorns.

Now, ruthless San Francisco gold baron Percival Dumay threatens everything Heck worked so hard to accomplish. With the help of crooked politicians and an army of tough prospectors, he aims to take Heck's gold, his land, and his life.

But this time, Dumay is fighting dirty against the wrong man.

Over the course of a drawn-out conflict, Dumay's demoralized men drift away, abandoning him, and Heck's supporters, whose friendship he has earned over years of helping others, trickle in.

In the final showdown, Heck outfights the professional killer, Frank Wedge, frees the valley, and chases off the last of the intruders.

Percival Dumay flees into the wilderness, where he meets his doom.

Heck looks optimistically to the future despite knowing that a frontier town growing this rapidly is bound to have troubles.

HECK'S STAND (HECK & HOPE #5) PICKS UP SEVERAL YEARS AFTER the events of *Heck's Gamble*. Heck's family has grown, as has Hope City. Folks have weathered the storms of life and prospered, but now, a severe drought grips the land, and Heck is about to embark on his most desperate adventure ever…

CAST OF CHARACTERS:

HECTOR "HECK" MARTIN: KENTUCKY-BORN MOUNTAIN MAN with big frontier spirit, former bareknuckle boxing champion of the West, tall lean and powerful with a black hair and blue eyes, tough yet compassionate.

HOPE MARTIN: HECK'S WIFE, KIND, IMPULSIVE, PLAYFUL, GOD-fearing, great with animals, a gifted nurse with auburn hair and green eyes.

HECTOR "TOR" MARTIN: HECK AND HOPE'S OLDEST BOY. HE loves his family and wants to follow his father everywhere.

SEEKER YATES, HECK'S ADOPTED BROTHER, A HALF-SHOSHONE orphan wise in the ways of the wilderness who had been wary and lonesome until he met Heck. Now a man grown, he is a formidable figure.

MR. MULLEN: HOPE'S FATHER, A FORMER BOXER, TOUGH YET quick to laugh, recently recovered from severe wounds sustained on the Oregon Trail, loves his family fiercely.

MRS. MULLEN: HOPE'S MOTHER, INTELLIGENT AND LOVING, sober-minded, follower of Jesus and often the voice of wisdom.

TOM MULLEN: HOPE'S BROTHER, A GIFTED LEATHERWORKER, husband of Amelia.

AMOS JOHNSON: A FRONTIER BARD SAVED BY HECK AND HOPE after a grizzly attack, travels the West chronicling the deeds of great men. After a long stay, he left Heck's Valley, headed for California and new stories.

BLACK CLOUD: SEEKER'S SHOSHONE UNCLE, WHO HELPED AVENGE the murder of his sister, Seeker's mother, by Sioux raiders.

JIM BRIDGER: THE FAMOUS MOUNTAIN MAN, HECK'S FRIEND.

TWO BITS: JIM BRIDGER'S SHOSHONE EMPLOYEE, WHO "WILL DO anything for two bits."

ABLE DEAN: HECK'S LAWYER.

DON VASQUEZ: THE CATTLEMAN WHO BOUGHT HECK'S NUGGET for a herd of longhorns, some top cattle horses, and the service of vaqueros.

MAJOR AVERY SCOTTSDALE: HECK'S OLD FRIEND FROM FORT Bent, now stationed at Fort Laramie.

DUSTY MAGUIRE: NEARLY KILLED BY DUMAY'S MEN, DUSTY remains a tough cowboy.

. . .

Shorty Potter: Another tough cowboy who proved his worth during the battle with Dumay.

The Emigrants

Doctor Michael "Doc" Skiff: broad-shouldered and bespectacled, Heck's best friend among the emigrants, a man of many talents, physician, pastor, fisherman, cook.

Titus Haines: widower, former wagon master, schoolmaster, and cavalry officer.

Amelia Mullen, Tom Mullen's wife and Titus Haines's daughter.

Susan Haines, Amelia's sister.

Sam Collins: assayer, helpful.

Myles Mason: furniture maker, undertaker.

. . .

Ray McLean: Australian jack-of-all-trades, former engineer and proofreader for a women's magazine, can fix anything.

Laticia Wolfe, a.k.a. "The Widow": emaciated but hard a tempered steel, she is proud that her son has grown into a strong, capable man.

Paul Wolfe: a young man who has grown strong thanks to the rigors of frontier life and help from Heck and Seeker.

Burt Bickle: freighter, hard worker, ambitious.

Abe Zale: young woodcutter with a can-do attitude.

A.J. Plum: talented blacksmith, stubborn, gets an idea and sticks to it. With him are his wife and three children, the oldest of which is nine-year-old Martin, a good little carpenter.

Gable Pillsbury: farmer.

Veronica Pillsbury: experienced midwife, Gable's wife, mother of two children.

. . .

FRANK PILLSBURY: FARMER, GABLE'S BROTHER, HUSBAND OF DOT, father of four children including thirteen-year-old Franky and eleven-year-old Mary.

WILL AYERS: CARPENTER.

CHAPTER 1

The buzzard swung in a slow circle, staring down at the man who lay motionless upon the stony, sunbaked ridge.

The buzzard, like most Westerners, did not care that the man's skin was dark brown.

The same could not be said for the two men who paused now in the dusty valley and stared up at the ridge.

Like the buzzard, they wanted the man dead. They had already done their best to achieve that goal, ambushing him two days earlier, when there were still four of them.

The black man had surprised them, however. Somehow, he had managed to survive the ambush, kill Bob Hazlett, and escape.

They had wounded him, though, and wounded his horse, and they would have finished him if night hadn't fallen.

They'd waited for daylight, found the blood trail, and tracked the man, but the only corpse they found was that of the horse.

The black man had stopped the bleeding and slipped away on foot into the night.

Again, they thought they had him. In country like this, a man on foot was buzzard bait.

But they didn't have him. Not yet. In fact, he'd proven downright wily.

And then, late the next day, he proved more than wily, killing Seymour from a distance and pinning them down until darkness fell.

Then, he slipped away again.

But he was hurt, horseless, and must be out of water by now.

These men were Southerners, and though they'd never owned slaves, they'd worked alongside them, and to them it was an offense beyond measure that a black man would dare to shoot one white man, let alone two.

At first, they'd just meant to kill and rob him. But now, they were on a noble mission to bring this murderous ex-slave to justice.

How he'd managed to evade them this long, they would never know. They just knew they had to stop him before he got to Petit Wells, because if he made it that far, he could hole up, and they would have a time getting to him… and the only water for miles.

But seeing the buzzard spin in slow circles, they reckoned the black man's luck had finally run out.

"Gotta be him up there," Dawkins said and licked his cracked lips.

"Yeah, I think he done expired."

"We'll just wait a touch. Get on back under the rim so he can't shoot us."

Gadson nodded. "He's uncommon good with that rifle."

So they got under cover and watched the buzzard, knowing if the man moved, the buzzard would break off.

Time passed—five minutes, ten, more—and instead of breaking off, the buzzard dropped to the ridge and disappeared.

"Let's get up there before that buzzard eats him all up," Dawkins said with a big grin, and they rode up the slope, laughing triumphantly.

The buzzard flew off as they rode uphill, but that was to be expected with their approach.

"Hope he's still alive so we can string him up and watch him kick."

"Yeah, well, dead's dead and justice will be served. What we ought to do is—"

Whatever plan Dawkins had been going to propose died as they topped the ridge, and a rifle round punched through his breastbone, exited his back, and burned across the arm of Gadson, who cursed and reined in with shock as the gunshot echoed off neighboring ridges.

Gadson lifted his rifle, but he was too late.

The black man, standing no more than twenty yards away, had already dropped his rifle and picked up a revolver.

Tricked! Gadson thought. *Tricked by a no good—*

The revolver barked, and Gadson's thoughts sheered away forever as a .44 caliber ball smashed through his forehead and killed him instantly.

Clarence Jefferson spat dryly and shook his head. He

reloaded the empty cylinder of his 1848 Colt Dragoon, then retrieved, checked, and reloaded his 1853 Barnett rifle.

It had been a gamble, laying there, baking in the sun, losing precious hydration as he waited for the buzzard to draw the men to him, but it had paid off.

And now, with two horses, Clarence would be able to make the thirty miles to Petit Wells.

But he'd have to hurry.

This whole drought-choked region was fixing to explode. The tribes had had enough of the invaders, and they didn't much care if those invaders were white or black.

Locally, the Sioux were on the warpath, and in this country, there was no more formidable enemy than a party of painted Sioux.

They were bred to this land and raised not only to fight but also to endure all manner of suffering: pain, heat, cold, hunger... anything and everything.

Clarence smiled grimly. *So were you,* he thought, looting the corpses of the men who'd tried to kill him. *So were you.*

A few moments later, he rode off on one bandit's horse, trailing the other, leaving their former riders as a thanks to the hungry buzzard.

CHAPTER 2

"Daddy has a treasure map!" the boy across the counter from Heck proclaimed proudly.

"Hush, Simon!" the boy's mother hissed.

Now, Heck understood.

Now, he understood why these folks were traveling late in the season, why they were going it alone, why they were heading south, and why they were determined to push on despite the drought and current state of Indian affairs, which was reminiscent of a freshly kicked ant hill.

The Horse Creek Treaty was dead.

First, tribes started crossing agreed-upon boundaries to hunt. The United States Government did nothing to protect the smaller tribes, did not deliver all they had promised, and stayed silent when emigrants and prospectors flooded in, encroaching on tribal lands, killing game, and hemming in buffalo with their rutted roads.

The tribes started striking back. As did the emigrants and the Army.

Across the West, things were heating up. And not just with the Indians.

It had been a scorching, rainless summer.

Heck's Valley had fared better than most of the country, thanks to its many springs and protective hills and forests, not to mention the ingenious cisterns and irrigation system created by the Australian women's magazine editor and jack-of-all-trades, Ray McLean.

But beyond the valley, the land gasped, baked brown and nearly lifeless beneath what seemed a cruel sun. As the world crumbled, dust filled the winds, cutting visibility and covering everything in choking silt.

And yet this man, this husband and father, was determined to follow a counterfeit map straight into destruction.

Heck shook his head. "Mister, if you take that route, the only treasure you'll end up hunting is water, and if you don't find it, you'll die."

The man stiffened at Heck's words. He was short and muscular with dark hair, dark eyes, and a short beard, and he stood now with his chest puffed out, reminding Heck of a rooster with its blood stirred.

"I'll be happy to remind you I didn't ask for advice," the man said. He half-turned and directed a withering look at his son, who reminded Heck of his oldest boy, Tor.

The man's son shifted from foot to foot and studied the floor.

The woman had her doubts, Heck could see.

But nonetheless, she lifted her chin and said, "We thank you for your concern, sir, but my husband knows what he's doing." She punctuated this assertion with a short nod, as if that closed the matter.

Her loyalty was understandable.

Commendable, even, if you ignored the fact that her stubborn, foolish husband was following a con man's map that was fixing to get them all killed.

"I don't make a habit of butting into folks' business," Heck said, "but even if you get lucky and the wells are full, the Indians—"

"We'll manage just fine," the man said, raising his voice. "And for your information, I am no stranger to fighting Indians."

The woman touched his arm. "Bruce," she said in a soft, coaxing voice, "I'm certain this nice man meant no harm. Let's not forget. We are here because we *need* supplies."

Heck heard her emphasize the word *need* and understood she was struggling with a new fear: that Heck might take offense and send them packing into the waterless wilderness with no supplies.

Which of course he would never do, no matter what the man said. Because denying someone help here was tantamount to murder.

Bruce nodded grimly and licked his lips as his eyes flicked across the well-stocked shelves of Badger's Trading Post.

"Mrs. Duncan is right. I meant no offense. We do need supplies."

Heck smiled. "And you'll have them, of course. You folks talk among yourselves and pick out what you need, and I'll see about getting your boy here a stick of hard candy."

"Well," Bruce Duncan said dubiously. "I don't know if—"

"On the house, of course," Heck hastened to say. "Would either of you like a piece of candy, too?"

The Duncans thanked him but declined his offer and started working their way around the store, marveling over its impressive inventory.

Heck pulled young Simon Duncan aside and held out the candy container to him.

The boy sheepishly accepted a peppermint stick. "Thank you, sir."

"You're welcome, Simon."

The boy's crooked grin again reminded Heck of his own son.

"You look a bit candy starved," Heck told him. "Why don't you go ahead and take another for the road?"

"Thank you, sir!"

"My pleasure," Heck said and added something he could not, in good conscience, neglect to say. "And son, if you run into Indian trouble and something bad happens to your folks, you stand up straight and tall, okay? You don't show an ounce of fear to those Indians. No matter what."

He did not explain that doing so and impressing the Indians would be the boy's only chance at survival if worse indeed came to worse.

The boy's eyes bulged, but he nodded solemnly. "Yes, sir."

Heck beamed at him, mussed his hair, and tucked a third peppermint stick in the boy's shirt pocket. "Good man."

CHAPTER 3

Heck finished rereading *Histories* by Herodotus, placed it on the bedside table, and stared for a moment at his beautiful wife, who lay sleeping beside him.

Even now, after all this time together, he could happily stare at her for minutes on end, fascinated by every line of her lovely face.

He felt so lucky, so blessed, to have Hope as his wife. She was the only woman in the whole world for him, and he would never cease wondering how he, a barefoot mountain boy from Kentucky, an orphan without two pennies to rub together, had managed to meet and eventually marry her.

Now, they had four children together.

Tor, Faith, and Jim slept across the room in a tangle of arms and legs and nightshirts.

Their fourth child remained in Hope's belly.

Glancing from his wife to his children and back to Hope, he wondered if he was about to make a mistake.

He blew out the candle and laid back to sleep. Dawn was only three hours off, and if he was going to do this thing, sleep might be downright scarce for the foreseeable future.

So he lay in the darkness and tried to still his mind.

It was no use.

He kept picturing the boy, Simon. Kept remembering his crooked smile.

Where were they now? South of here by a stretch.

Was he already too late?

Had the boy even had a chance to finish his peppermint sticks?

Heck rose, moving slowly and silently as not to wake his wife.

He crossed the room, cutting through a shaft of moonlight, and stared down at his three children.

They slumbered deeply, all worn out from yet another day of work and play.

His heart swelled to the bursting.

How he loved them.

"We'll be okay, Heck," Hope's voice called from their bed.

He turned toward her shadowy shape. "Sorry I woke you."

"I haven't been sleeping. Not really. I've been resting… and waiting."

"Waiting for what?"

"To tell you what I just told you. We'll be all right. You're going, aren't you?"

Heck took a deep breath, stared out the window, and exhaled slowly. "Yeah, I'm going."

"I knew you would. I knew as soon as those people left."

He nodded. "They'll die out there."

"Yes, they will."

"I wish they'd listened."

"So do I," Hope said. "Maybe now, after seeing more of the country…"

"That's what I'm hoping. Trouble is, this land doesn't like to give second chances. That Bruce Duncan is stubborn. If he sees what it'll take to change his mind, I reckon it'll be the last thing he ever sees."

"Why go, then?"

"You know why."

"In case you can save them."

"Yes, in case I can save them."

"It's the boy, isn't it?"

"It's all of them, but yeah, mostly it's him."

"He looks a little bit like Tor."

"He does. Especially when he grins."

"Which he was bound to do, what with you giving him all that free candy."

Heck chuckled. "What good is having a store if you can't give a kid free candy from time to time?"

"You're a good man, Heck Martin."

"And you're a good woman, Hope Martin."

But as he stared down at his sleeping children, he had to wonder if he was indeed a good man.

Did a good man put his own wife and children at risk to go after strangers that didn't even want saving?

He didn't know the answer to that. He didn't even know if there was an answer.

He only knew that he had no choice. It was his nature, and he had to try.

"Who are you taking with you?" Hope asked.

"No one. I'll travel faster and quieter that way."

Hope was silent for a moment, and he thought she might question his logic, but what she said was, "Come back to bed, my love. If you're going to travel, I need a proper goodbye while the children are still sleeping."

CHAPTER 4

Cody Woodson hid high above the pool, stretched out atop a shelf where two of the huge boulders met each other and the rougher stone of hill behind Petit Wells. Luckily, the hill also provided an overhang that sheltered him from the blistering sun overhead.

He had food and two full canteens and a good deal of shot and powder. If need be, he could hide here for days.

If only he'd been able to get Annie up here, too, but that, of course, was impossible.

The mare grazed happily down by the pool.

Cody was tall for sixteen, nearly five feet ten inches, and wiry with muscle from a life of toil and travel.

This spring, he'd left Texas with three men, friends of his late father—God rest his soul—and headed west, bound for fame and fortune.

Only the would-be prospectors had found neither of those things.

The trip had been hard on the older men, especially with the drought, and they had begun to regret coming west.

Not Cody.

Through all the difficulties, he held fast to his dream. Even now, even here, hiding alone upon this rock at the heart of a deadly wasteland, he clung to the hope of a better life.

He was young and strong and liked to work. It didn't matter to him whether he panned for gold, cut wood, or drove cattle. He had struck out to make his way in the world, and that was still, despite this unfortunate turn of events, what he planned to do.

Three days earlier, Cody woke early, as was his habit, and went out before first light to hunt, hoping fresh meat might strengthen his friends and lift their spirits.

Shots and screaming drew him back to camp.

If there had been fewer Indians, he would have opened fire, especially if it might have saved the others.

But there were two dozen Indians, and Cody was too late to save anyone.

So he'd slipped away and hightailed it for this place, Petit Wells. Finding the cluster of boulders deserted, he gathered his things, dismounted straight onto the big stones, and climbed to this spot, leaving no tracks on the ground and no marks, he hoped, on the boulders themselves.

He left Annie below, knowing she would stick close to the tank. She seemed happy enough down there with plenty of grass and water.

He had no doubt the Indians would come and find her. Since he'd left no tracks on the ground, however, he hoped they would assume Annie had run off on her own and found water.

If, on the other hand, they searched for him, he would fight tooth and nail. This was a perfect position. Yes, they would get him eventually but not before he took many of them with him.

Despite this grim promise to himself, Cody was optimistic by nature, and he still believed in his future, a future far from this lifeless place, a future with his own plot of ground, crops, stock, a wife, and children—all the things that made a man complete.

No one came that first day.

Or the second.

Now, at noon of the third day, he was thinking of leaving his perch.

He didn't have to. Not yet.

He had been rationing his food and water, of course. Food was not a problem, not really. He still had some jerky and hard-tack, and he had gone without food many times as a child. Many, many times.

But water was another story. A man could not live without water, and he was down to half a canteen.

Perhaps he could tie a bit of rope to his canteen, lower it to the dark pool, and bring it back up, getting water without leaving tracks. Even if he managed to fill it halfway, he—

The sound of approaching hoofbeats shattered his thoughts.

Cody eased back from the edge and checked his rifle, heart pounding.

This is it, he thought, hearing the Indians ride into the enclosure. *Now, you hide or make your stand.*

But the riders laughed loudly—something he would never expect from Indians—and one of the men shouted, "We made it. And look, Pete, just like I told you, plenty of water!"

Relief washed over Cody. These were white men.

But life had tempered Cody's optimism and made him wary, so he didn't go hollering down to the newcomers.

He figured he'd just wait a moment. You can learn a lot about men by listening to them talk—especially if they don't know you're listening.

He inched cautiously forward and peered down.

There were two men. One large, one small. Soldiers, by their uniforms.

But soldiers like Cody had never seen before. Dirty, ragged, and unshaven, they had clearly been in the wilderness for some time.

The men dismounted and drank alongside their animals.

"Look, Hank," the small one said, pointing across the pool to where Annie blinked at them from the shade. "A horse!"

Hank jumped to his feet. A second later, a rifle was in his big hands, and he was sweeping its barrel in every direction, ready for trouble. He moved with shocking speed, given his size.

"Hello?" Hank called. "Anybody here?"

Cody remained silent.

"I don't see nobody," Pete said. Now he had a rifle, too.

"Well, let's just have a look around," Hank said, turning slowly.

"You don't think it's somebody from the fort, do you? Somebody hunting us? That Gentry, he won't quit. Remember when the other kid deserted, the one with the—"

"Shut up, Pete," Hank growled. "It ain't nobody from the fort. How would they get here before us? They were all sleeping when we lit out. Besides, look at the horse, look at the saddle. Do they look government issue to you?"

"Where's the rider?" Pete asked.

Hank studied the ground. "Might not be a rider. I don't see no tracks. Might be the rider's dead."

"If he's dead, where is he?"

"Somewhere. How should I know? Maybe miles off."

"Well then, what's his horse doing here?"

"Animals have a way of finding water."

"You think maybe?" Pete asked.

Hank ignored the question and called out again, even louder than before. "Hello? Anybody here? My name's Hank, and this here is Pete. We're good men, soldiers. Hello?"

Cody considered answering. He could go down, introduce himself, and have some water.

But his gut told him to stay quiet.

These men were running from something. It sounded like they had deserted their posts.

If so, they were likely not only bad soldiers but also bad men. Desperate men. The type of men who might kill a kid in the desert for his horse and rifle and whatever else he might have.

So Cody settled in to wait… and kept his rifle close.

CHAPTER 5

T he forest held its breath.

Among its gnarled, stunted trees, an unnatural silence reigned as a lone man moved with exquisite slowness, stepping carefully, and hating even the soft sounds of his own breathing in the close air, which had grown stifling with the unrelenting heat.

Short, slender, and muscular, Bruce Duncan was neither old nor young. No silver yet streaked his black hair or beard, but his hands were deeply calloused, and his dark eyes roved the forest warily.

A Bowie knife rode one hip. Shot and powder rode the other.

Bruce gripped a .54 caliber Harpers Ferry Model 1841 muzzleloader, better known on the frontier as a Mississippi rifle.

Weighing nine pounds unloaded, the rifle was heavy, but Bruce was strong from a lifetime of farming, and the Mississippi's power and 1,100-yard range justified the extra weight.

He was glad for it in this eerie forest.

The thought brought a grim smile to his face.

Eerie?

Was he a child to be scared by silence and strange trees?

No, he was not.

But even as he scoffed at the notion, he couldn't shake the sense of menace.

It was all because of the tall man, of course, the one back at the trading post. His words had fallen like bitter rain across Bruce's mind, sunk into his thoughts, and watered seeds of doubt he hadn't even known were buried there.

All Bruce's life, he had been a simple, efficient, straightforward man. Presented with a situation, he would observe, consider his options, make a choice, devise a plan, prepare, and carry on without wavering until he had seen it through.

This had worked for him throughout his life, whether he was buying land, raising crops, or courting Mabel.

But the tall man's words had watered Bruce's secret doubts, and over the three days since leaving Hope City, they had sprung up, cluttering his thoughts like a tangle of dark thistles.

Bruce had traded their life savings for the treasure map, then sold the farm and most of the stock and equipment to buy the schooner and supplies.

The map had seemed like the opportunity of a lifetime. Once he'd made his decision, he'd never looked back.

Until the tall man.

It wasn't just the man's words. It was his confidence, too, his obvious concern for Bruce and his family.

Was the man right?

Had Bruce been a fool? Had he blundered everything?

Was he leading his beloved family toward treasure or destruction?

Mabel had her doubts, he knew, but she was a good woman and a fine wife—brave and patient and trusting—and she had said nothing.

She and Simon traveled in the wagon a short distance behind him. He hated leaving them alone like that, but at least this way, he could scout ahead.

Picturing their faces, he felt a pang of protectiveness and squashed his doubts.

He had made his choice. They were on their way. The only thing to do now was see it through and hope for the best.

For all he knew, the tall man had simply been trying to frighten them for the fun of it.

Whatever the case, he cast off these thoughts, knowing they could only cloud his senses.

And here, in this wild place, he must remain alert for danger.

So onward he moved, stepping cautiously, making almost no noise whatsoever, scanning the trees and bushes and trail, listening for any sound, no matter how slight.

But there were no sounds. Unnatural silence gripped the forest and draped a frigid blanket of menace over Bruce.

Suddenly, every fiber of his body quivered like a rabbit's nose, sensing danger.

He stopped, half crouching, eyes wide, nostrils flaring, ears straining, straining, straining.

And then, all at once, he heard a muffled thump and the unmistakable twang of a bowstring.

He hunched defensively, but the arrow streaked across the trail at an erratic angle.

With a snapping of branches, a man who had been hiding behind the trailside bushes spilled into view.

The Indian lay half in, half out of the bushes, and obviously quite dead, given the tomahawk jutting from the back of his head.

Who had swung the tomahawk?

Bruce shouldered his rifle, ready to fire into the bushes.

"Don't shoot," a deep voice said, and a huge man clad in buckskins stepped from the thicket and nonchalantly pulled the axe from the dead man's head.

Bruce stared in disbelief.

It was him.

"You can put down the rifle," the man said. "He was alone."

Bruce lowered the rifle. "I know you. From the trading post."

The tall man nodded and wiped the blade of the tomahawk before hanging it once more from his heavy leather belt.

"What are you doing here?" Bruce asked, suddenly wary. Had the tall man come for the treasure?

Bruce considered lifting his rifle again, putting it on the man to disarm and interrogate him.

The tall man grinned wolfishly. "Don't do anything stupid, Mr. Duncan. I just saved your life. If I'd wanted your map, I would have let him kill you before taking him out. Relax. I'm here to help. Now, has this brought you to your senses? Are you ready to turn around?"

CHAPTER 6

Count Viktor Karpov cursed in his mother tongue, drawing bitter laughter from his wife, Natalia, whose mare looked even more exhausted than his own gelding.

Meanwhile, Becky's pony looked much fresher, as did the young, well-formed blonde herself. Viktor had procured the pony at Fort Laramie, where the rest of the wagon train had halted, struck by cowardice.

The pony wasn't just fresher than the horses. It was born and bred to this godforsaken land.

How Viktor hated America. And he hated no portion of it more than the West.

The spaces were so vast, so empty.

At least while hunting the sprawling taiga of home, you occasionally stumbled across beautiful animals to shoot or a village where you might have some fun.

Here in this dusty wasteland, they saw neither man nor game. They hadn't even had a chance to shoot any of the famous American savages, something Viktor had been longing to do.

What was the sense of making such a brutal trek if you couldn't at least kill a few Indians?

But of course, he knew very well the sense behind making this trip. Given the current state of things and what he planned to achieve, a trek across the wilderness was his only choice.

His money was nearly out.

He couldn't afford to book passage on a ship to California for himself and the countess, let alone Becky.

And he would not go to California without Becky.

Like the pony she rode, Becky was a low-born American creature, but unlike the pony, Becky was also a creature of exquisite beauty, a study in bouncing curves crowned in golden curls.

Which was why a pearl necklace now glimmered around her peasant throat.

Once he reached California, Becky would be his mistress.

Becky did not understand this, of course. Viktor and Natalia had plucked her straight from the family farm, where she had worked alongside numerous brothers and sisters. A juicy piece of fruit, she was, and deliciously naïve.

She was also maddeningly chaste, insisting on privacy whenever she bathed or dressed, but that would change in time.

For now, she believed that Viktor and his wife were merely friendly, and that they had hired her on as a traveling companion with no set duties, like a pair of happy buffoons who had recognized something so special in her that they were delighted to pay her for nothing.

But in time, Viktor would have every penny's worth.

As would Natalia, who viewed Becky less as a mistress and more as a breeder. Coming from aristocracy, Natalia understood the notion of mistresses, which were to be expected among the upper class, as well as the importance of Viktor producing an heir.

And because her own sister had died in labor, Natalia wanted nothing of pregnancy or producing heirs. She would carry on as the Countess. Becky could bear the children.

Which suited Viktor just fine.

He liked peasant girls. He would never have married one, of course—an absurd idea—but since boyhood, he had enjoyed forcing his father's serving girls to honor his every whim.

Despite his fondness for peasant girls, Viktor would not live among commoners. Not solely, anyway.

He needed to live among other gentlemen and their ladies, people like him, people of breeding and education, who understood decorum and the finer things in life.

Among such people he could rise again.

Which meant settling in New York, New Orleans, or California.

There were too many Russians in New York, however, too many people who knew Viktor's story, too many people who knew his father and might report back to the good general.

And Viktor had resolved to have no further contact with his father until he had made a new name for himself along with a new fortune.

He would not negotiate from a position of weakness, not with his father. He must first make himself General Karpov's equal.

So New York, with all its Russians, could not be the answer.

Neither could New Orleans. He had visited the bustling city and wallowed for a time in its diversions, but the air was bad, damp, and full of unpleasant smells, and Natalia developed a cough, so they departed immediately, ready to be rid of the riotous, rotting city.

California, then, was the answer.

Spaniards of pure blood and great wealth yet lived in California, as did many newly rich prospectors and businessmen.

Viktor spoke passable Spanish and understood the Spaniards, having lived in both Madrid and Valencia. Among these people, he could make a fresh start.

The others, the *nouveau riche,* he would endure because their wealth was vast, and like other newly rich persons the world over, they would be ripe for the taking.

First, he would sell to them the items within the lockbox he had taken from his father's estate in Russia. These men, who now ruled unthinkable fortunes and reportedly paid a dollar for a slice of bread and two dollars for a slice of *buttered* bread, would certainly pay truly exorbitant amounts for such treasures.

So while Viktor was running very low on cash, he was far from destitute. The lockbox held a fortune of gems and jewelry, things his father had taken through conquest and connection, things for which there were no buyers in the blasted vastness between New York and California.

Once he reached California and sold some of his precious stones and pieces of jewelry, he would purchase an estate, hire servants, and bend Becky to his will.

Ensconced on a beautiful estate with his presentable wife, luscious mistress, a competent staff, and an heir, he would begin a new life among the Spanish nobility, a life that would one day lift him to a station equal to or greater than that of his father.

And once he had achieved that station, he would contact the General and negotiate from a position of strength.

So that was why he, Natalia, and Becky were undergoing this awful trek.

And, of course, he still hoped to shoot some Indians.

For now, however, they must endure, riding far enough in front of the three wagons to avoid choking on their dust—but not far enough away that the freighters might abscond with their possessions.

He carried the lockbox on his horse, of course, and the wagons were mostly loaded with Natalia's clothing and furniture, but they also held their food and water barrels, and without those things, they would surely die.

And that, he refused to do. Dying here, upon this American wasteland would be beneath him, and Viktor still had much to do.

CHAPTER 7

Heck watched Bruce Duncan stand a little straighter. For just a second, there had been a flicker of indecision in his eyes—the man thinking, making connections, teetering on the edge of understanding—but then his eyes hardened, and he shook his head.

"It's gonna take more than one Injun to turn us back."

"Even though that Indian nearly killed you?"

"I would have taken care of him."

"No, you wouldn't have. He was going to shoot you in the back."

"Well, I thank you for stopping him. I will have to be more careful."

"Careful likely won't come into it. This man was Sioux. The Sioux are very intelligent, very organized."

"They're savages."

Heck spread his hands. "They're different. I won't argue that they aren't brutal because they are. But mostly they're different.

They're not white folks dressed up in costumes. They have their own ways, their own values."

"They torture people."

"Yes, they do. But you can't afford to think of them as stupid brutes. Frankly, you got lucky."

"I already thanked you."

"Not just because I was here. You're lucky there was just one of them. That was a fluke. Before long, though, he'll be missed. And then the Sioux will come for you. They won't come one at a time, and they won't come in a whooping rush. They'll come for you in the way that suits the moment, when they have the best chance of taking you without sustaining losses themselves. They are as cunning as they are ferocious."

"I'll be ready."

Heck frowned. He didn't like to tell another man his business, but this wasn't just about Bruce. "And what about your family? Are they ready to face a dozen Sioux warriors?"

Bruce said nothing for a second, and Heck could see that he was thinking again. Then he spat, overcome by stubbornness. "We'll be all right."

"No," Heck said. "No, you won't be all right."

How could he make Bruce Duncan understand the situation? If saving him from certain death wouldn't do it, what would?

They both turned as the wagon rolled into view.

Mrs. Duncan's face registered shock at the sight of Heck, but she recovered quickly, apparently recognizing him—or at least understanding he posed no danger.

Beside her, the boy Simon grinned and waved.

Heck nodded.

"Good afternoon, sir," Mrs. Duncan said, offering a pretty smile. Then she spotted the dead man and gasped. "What happened?"

"That Injun was fixing to shoot me in the back, but then…"

Bruce Duncan trailed off then shook his head as if frustrated with himself. "You saved my life, and I never even asked your name."

Heck stuck out a hand. "I'm Heck Martin."

"Bruce Duncan." The farmer looked Heck in the eye and shook firmly. "This is my wife, Mabel, and my son, Simon."

Heck nodded. "Nice to see you folks again."

The boy, who had been staring with huge eyes at the dead man, turned toward Heck with a look of awe.

Mabel Duncan said, "Mr. Martin, we can't thank you enough for what you've done. Can I at least offer you a meal and some coffee?"

"That would be real nice, ma'am," Heck said. "Thank you. But I don't reckon we ought to tarry here. This man's tribe will be hunting him. And then, when they find him, they'll be hunting you."

"Oh," Mrs. Duncan said, and lifted a hand to her mouth. "Yes, of course."

"Why don't you folks come on back to Hope City?" Heck said. "We have plenty of room, plenty of water, plenty of food. You can be my guests. You won't want for anything. You can wait out the drought and the Indian trouble and figure out what you want to do."

Mrs. Duncan smiled brightly. "Why that's very kind of you, Mr. Martin."

But then, as she looked at her husband, her face fell.

Bruce Duncan looked more stubborn than ever. "As I already told you, Mr. Martin, we are pushing on. You're more than welcome to a meal, but we'll be cooking it south of here, not north. We didn't come all this way to quit."

Heck glanced between the Duncans.

Bruce had come to his decision and would not waver. At least not now, not here, and not based on anything Heck might say.

Mrs. Duncan, on the other hand, wanted to head back to Hope City. That was obvious.But he could see she would not question her husband, especially not in front of Heck.

He wondered, however, if she might speak candidly with Bruce later, when they were alone. With a little time and privacy, she might sway her husband.

Heck had no way of knowing. But he had to give her the opportunity. Otherwise, these folks were rolling straight into death.

Finally, he considered the boy.

Young Simon Duncan sure did look like Tor. Especially that crooked grin.

"All right," Heck said. "I'll get you folks to Petit Wells. But then I'll turn back. I have my own family to think of."

CHAPTER 8

"Count Karpov?" Becky asked. "Shouldn't we be able to see the wagons by now?"

Viktor Karpov cursed, realizing that he'd been so lost in dreams of California and the new life he meant to build there that he had completely lost track of the wagons.

A mistake his father, the General, would never have made.

The thought filled him with bitter frustration.

Riding ahead of the wagons, avoiding their dust, had been intelligent.

But Becky was correct.

The wagons were supposed to stay fifty to one hundred yards behind them. Where were they?

He knew where they were, of course. The freighters had run off with his possessions, with all the water, leaving Viktor and his women to die of thirst.

"Stay here," he growled, turning the gelding.

"Where are you going, darling?" Natalia asked.

"I'm going to catch those thieves," he snapped, his blood heating for combat.

"But there are three of them and only one of you," Becky said, her face twisted with fear.

"Do not fear, my girl," Natalia said. "The Count has experience in such matters."

Viktor nodded. "And even if I didn't, they have our water. I must recapture it. No matter the danger."

He rode off, moving quickly but not too quickly. He couldn't afford to push the gelding, or it might drop dead. In country like this, a man would not fare well on foot.

A curious thing happened as Viktor rode his back trail. He realized he was excited. Realized, in fact, that he was smiling with anticipation.

Other than a couple of quick duels—no, three... he had momentarily forgotten the drunken Frenchman in New Orleans—Viktor had not seen combat since coming to America several months earlier.

Now, he thought, letting the thrill tickle over him, now, he would show these traitorous thieves how a real man fought.

Though he hoped he wouldn't have to kill all of them. Who would drive his wagons?

Reaching down, he unfastened the hammer loop, freeing his .36 caliber Colt Navy but leaving it holstered. Then he drew the 1853 Enfield from its scabbard.

Approaching the rise, he slowed his horse, remembering the long stretch of open scrubland that lay beyond. He did not wish to reveal his position or intention until he had pulled the trigger.

So Viktor stopped the horse midway up the slope and dismounted. Crouching low, he hurried uphill on foot.

He crawled the last few feet and peeked cautiously over the edge, meaning to read the situation and choose his first target.

Metcalf, probably.

He'd seen the man take a deer at two hundred yards. Best to get him out of the mix as quickly as—

His mind froze when he observed the scene on the other side.

Metcalf was no longer a concern.

The teamster lay motionless on the ground. His back bristled with arrows.

Dobson was also dead.

Several Indians had gathered around Miller, whose screams carried faintly across the scrubland, chilling Viktor's blood.

Additional savages clambered into the wagons and scampered back out with armloads of supplies like so many ants sieging a picnic basket.

Looking down at Dobson and Metcalf's corpses and hearing Miller's screams, Viktor thought, *Thank goodness. Thank goodness I have the gems with me!*

Moving swiftly and silently, he descended the slope again, mounted the gelding, and hurried back to the women.

The Indians would be coming for them.

They had to race to Petit Wells.

CHAPTER 9

"Howdy," the man pointing the rifle at Heck said.

Heck reined in, considered going for his Colt, and quickly thought better of it.

The man had been laying for them behind the low ridge. At this range—perhaps fifty yards—he'd have to be an awfully poor shot to miss with that rifle.

And from the looks of him, he'd been around. He was a tough-looking black man in filthy buckskins stained with sweat and blood, and a floppy, wide-brimmed hat.

"Howdy," Heck replied.

Behind him, the wagon stopped.

Bruce Duncan's voice demanded, "What do you want?"

"We just want to talk to you," a second man said from behind them.

Heck turned as the man emerged from a boulder to their rear.

For as rough as the black man looked, this man looked rougher still. He was a soldier—a sergeant, judging by his insignia—with gray hair, a limp, and a uniform that had seen far better days.

One sleeve had been cut away. That arm was wrapped in bloody bandages but seemed to be working well, judging by the steady way it gripped the rifle he was pointing at them.

"All right," Heck said, focusing on this man for a moment. "Talk."

"Have you folks seen a couple of soldiers?"

"Just you," Heck said. "But it looks like there's been a fair amount of traffic through here lately."

"Of course, maybe they ditched their uniforms," the sergeant said, "then robbed some poor soul and hid their treason beneath civilian clothes. Have you seen two men traveling together, one large, one small?"

Heck shook his head. "What did they do, desert?"

"That's right," the sergeant said, lowering his rifle. "But they didn't just desert. They abandoned their posts, left us vulnerable to attack. And when that attack came, the Indians nearly finished us."

"That's pretty low," Heck said.

The sergeant nodded then lifted his chin a little, his eyes burning with purpose. "I'm the last man standing, and I will bring Pipher and Twill to justice if it's the last thing I do."

"Understandable. You out of Laramie?"

"Yes, I am," the sergeant said. "Name's Sergeant Davis Gentry."

"Nice to meet you, Sergeant. My name's Heck Martin. You might know a friend of mine, Avery Scottsdale."

"If you're a friend of Major Scottsdale, I'm pleased to meet you, sir. He's a good man."

"Yes, he is," Heck agreed.

"Heck Martin," the black man said amiably. "I've heard stories about you. Truth to be told, they sounded like tall tales."

Heck turned to the man, who was descending the short slope now and no longer pointing a rifle in their direction.

"They might have been tall tales," Heck said. "Folks have a way of exaggerating."

"Well, they didn't exaggerate your size. You're a biggun, Heck." The man held out his hand, and they shook. "Name's Clarence Jefferson."

"Nice to meet you, Clarence. This is Bruce Duncan, his wife, Mabel, and their boy, Simon."

Clarence shook hands with Bruce, tipped his hat to Mabel, and grinned at Simon, who smiled back at him.

"I would've died if it weren't for Clarence," Sergeant Gentry said. "The day before I met him, my horse gave out. That night, I ran out of water. When Clarence found me, I was staggering. But he gave me a horse and a canteen, so my mission continues."

"This is rough country," Clarence said. "I'm surprised to see a family, given the state of things. The tribes are out for blood."

Heck said nothing and turned to Bruce.

"We're managing fine," Bruce said. "Just fine."

"Folks heading for Petit Wells, I suppose?" Clarence asked.

"That's right," Heck said. "You coming or going?"

"Going," Sergeant Gentry said. "Hoping to find those deserters there."

Heck turned to Clarence. "You hunting these men, too?"

"Me? No, sir. I'm not hunting men, I'm hunting water."

"You are out of water?" Mabel said. "We have a barrel in the wagon."

Bruce shot his wife an irritated look but said nothing.

"I'd be much obliged, ma'am," Clarence said. "I'm down to my last drops and have been rationing hard for a couple of days now."

"I'd be much obliged, too, ma'am," Sergeant Gentry said.

As the men filled their canteens, Heck said, "Well, if we're all heading to Petit Wells, let's travel together. We still have a few miles to go. A lot can happen in that space."

"That it can," Clarence said, and took a drink. "Ah. Been choking on dust for days. I sure do appreciate that, ma'am."

"Our pleasure, I'm sure," Mabel said.

"Since you're friends with Major Scottsdale," Sergeant Gentry said, "maybe you can help me apprehend the deserters if we find them at Petit Wells."

"Maybe," Heck said. No stranger to this country, he'd never stopped scanning the landscape. Now he pointed to where three columns of black smoke rose from the ridged land between them and Petit Wells. "But I reckon if we're lucky enough to make it to the wells, we're gonna need every man and every gun we can get."

CHAPTER 10

Becky Bonneville had never been so frightened as she was now, racing away from the Indians who had overtaken the wagons.

Thank goodness she was with the Count.

He was so strong, so confident. And the Countess said he was a fighting man, a man with no fear of the Indians.

Though she hated to slow Petunia, she did. Otherwise, she would leave the Count and Countess alone.

And Becky did not want to be alone in this dry and dusty land of death.

Stay calm, she told herself. *The count will protect you.*

And later, after they were safe in California, she would be able to share their amazing tale of escape.

If they escaped…

Becky glanced back over her shoulder and was horrified to see smoke rising in their wake, back beyond the hill where the wagons had stopped.

What had happened to those men, the drivers?

She hadn't known them, not really, but she'd spoken to each man at some point. Picturing their faces filled her with fear and loathing. Those poor men...

But then the Count was beside her, matching her stride for stride, his face cool and confident though a bit stern as always.

He pointed to where the trail ahead wrapped around a set of large boulders clustered together at the foot of a sandy ridge. "That's Petit Wells. We'll hide within those stones."

"But the Indians will track us there."

The Count smiled darkly. He certainly was handsome. "Then we will fight them."

"Yes, sir," Becky said and rode for the boulders while the Count dropped back to ride alongside the Countess.

Even now, with their lives in peril, Becky felt a wave of admiration. What a wonderful man the Count was to shield and comfort his wife.

If Becky ever got out of this mess alive—*you will*, she told herself; *thanks to the Count, you will*—she hoped she could find herself a brave, attentive husband like the Count.

Not that she could dream of marrying someone so hand-some, wealthy, or important as the Count. She was, after all, just a seventeen-year-old girl straight off the farm.

Why would a great man like the Count be interested in a plain farm girl like her?

And then, suddenly, against all odds, Becky was stifling laughter. Here she was, running for her life from Indians, and daydreaming about meeting the right husband.

Ridiculous!

But then she risked another look over her shoulder, saw the

plumes of smoke rising darkly into the air, and all the laughter went out of her.

Filled with fresh fear, she urged Petunia forward, and the brave little pony flew over the hard, dusty ground, carrying her swiftly toward the boulders and, she hoped, safety.

A moment later, she slowed the pony, approaching the circle of smooth, reddish boulders which towered thirty feet into the air.

How had these massive stones even gotten here? They looked as if God Himself had placed them here in a circle, perhaps to make Himself a fire ring.

The main trail curved away alongside the boulders, continuing toward the southwest.

Remembering the Count's orders, Becky instead followed the narrower trail that disappeared between two of the towering rocks.

Then, she was inside the circle, wide-eyed with surprise at the explosion of color within—trees, shrubs, and grasses flourishing alongside the large pool at the back of the space within the stones—and at the two men who stood there pointing rifles at her.

"Oh my goodness," Becky said, reining Petunia to a stop. "Please don't shoot."

"Sorry, ma'am," the smaller of the men said, lowering his rifle. "We thought maybe you was an Injun or… someone else."

With a flash of relief, Becky realized these men were soldiers. Their uniforms were in disarray, but yes, they were soldiers, thank goodness, not brigands.

But the bigger man—and he was very large indeed—smiled nastily. "No ma'am, we sure won't shoot a pretty lady like you."

Becky wished he wouldn't look at her that way and wished even more that he would lower his rifle.

Then, the Count and Countess rode in behind her, and the men swung the barrels in their direction.

"What is the meaning of this?" the Count demanded. He sounded very angry. "Put down those rifles at once."

"You talk funny," the smaller man said, not lowering his rifle this time.

"Sounds Russian to me," the bigger man said.

"That is correct, sir," the Countess said. "I am Countess Natalia Karpov of St. Petersburg, and this is my husband, the esteemed Count Viktor Karpov."

Becky was thrilled to hear the authority in the Countess's voice. She was so brave and proud and—

"Not out here, you ain't," the big man said, and as he studied the Countess, his nasty grin returned. "Out here, he's just a man, and you're just a woman. A mighty fine-looking woman at that. Now, Count Russian, move real slow and hand my partner that rifle of yours, butt first, if you please. And we'll have that leg iron, too, and any other guns you're packing."

"I most certainly will not surrender my weapons," the Count said. "There are Indians out there. In fact, they might arrive any moment. They killed our men and burned our wagons."

"Pity," the big man said. "Now, give up the guns, or I'll put a bullet right through your royal heart."

Becky gasped. This was all wrong. How could it be possible? Soldiers were supposed to protect frontiersmen, not threaten them.

And this was no idle threat. She could see that. She hoped the Count could see it, too, hoped he didn't do anything—

"Put down the rifles," a voice said from above, startling Becky badly.

Everyone jerked at the new voice, and when they looked up, they saw the face of a young man lying in the boulders twenty feet above them, sighting down a rifle that was trained on the big soldier.

"I won't tell you twice," the young man said.

The soldiers did as they were told.

The smaller of the pair demanded, "Who are you? Where did you come from?"

"My name's Cody Woodson," the young man said and smiled down at them—smiled directly at Becky, in fact.

Her face grew hot at the realization. Mr. Cody Woodson had a very nice smile, she thought.

"I've been up here since before you two rode in," Cody said, "listening and waiting. Now, you folks gotta quit your bickering because the Count is right. There are riders coming. I can see their dust from up here."

CHAPTER 11

They angled southwest, staying to one side of the smoke while still drawing closer to Petit Wells.

Heck had suggested ditching the wagon, which pitched a cloud of dust that would announce their location for miles around, but Bruce unsurprisingly refused.

"Well, we'd better hurry, then," Heck said. "I'm hoping the Indians found some whiskey in those wagons they're burning. Otherwise, we are in a lot of trouble."

"Do you really think it's wagons burning, Mr. Martin?" Mabel asked.

"What else could burn like that out here?" Heck asked. "It's wagons. I just hope the owners had sense enough to abandon them before the Indians showed up."

They set off at a brisk pace.

Heck rode in front.

Clarence rode beside him.

They both scanned the surrounding country, and when they spoke, it was without looking at one another.

"These people kin to you?" Clarence asked.

"They are not. I suppose you're wondering why I'm riding with them."

"I figure you took pity."

"Basically. They passed through my place a few days back."

"You got the trading post, right? Hope City and all that?"

"That's right."

"Like I said, I've heard stories. They say a few years back, you stood off a whole army."

"Wasn't much of an army, and I had help."

"Okay. So these folks come to your trading post?"

"Right. Said they were coming this way. I warned them. Told them about the country, the lack of water, the Indians."

"But that fella Bruce wouldn't hear it?"

"You catch on fast, Clarence."

"Any fool with two eyes can see he's stubborn as a mule."

"You're not wrong."

"And he's not alone."

"Again, you catch on quick, Clarence."

"Well, let's just see how quick I catch on. So they come by, you warn them, he tells you to go climb a tree."

Heck chuckled. "Something like that."

"Then you get thinking about that woman and her boy."

"Right so far."

"And you set out with them, like an escort."

"Almost right. I didn't set out until they had already gone down the trail a ways. Caught up just in time. A lone Sioux was fixing to shoot Bruce in the back."

Now, Clarence did look at Heck, his face contorted with surprise. "You saved Bruce's life like that, and he still wouldn't turn around?"

"Not even when I offered them free room and board through the winter."

"That's a mighty generous offer."

"God blessed me with plenty. I promised the Duncans I'd get them as far as Petit Wells. After that, I'm heading home. You want to ride along, I'll offer you the same setup."

"I appreciate that. We survive this, I might just take you up on that offer. I been riding hard and living lean for a long time. Might be nice to hole up for a spell."

"Only thing is, you gotta work. That's my one rule in Hope City. Everybody works."

"Work," Clarence laughed. "If there's one thing I can do, it's work. You bring out your two best men, I'll work them both into the ground. Bet on it."

"Well, I was just being neighborly," Heck said, "but it sounds like I might've stumbled across a good thing."

"We'll see about that. First, I'd guess we got some fighting to do."

"I reckon you're right."

"In that case," Clarence said, "I hope some of them tall tales really are true. I hear you fight like two devils."

They rode for a few miles in silence.

Behind them, Sergeant Gentry and the Duncans followed, the wagon kicking up a constant plume of dust.

It was only a matter of time before that dust drew trouble.

Finally, as they descended into a valley blurred by heat waves, Heck spotted the rider sitting atop a neighboring ridge.

"Indian," Clarence remarked a second later.

"I see him."

"You don't reckon he's alone, do you?"

"No, sir. I don't reckon he is, not all painted up like that."

"Sioux?"

"Little hard to say from this distance, but if I had to guess, yeah, I'd say he's Sioux."

"That's not good news."

"No, it's not."

Glancing back, he realized neither the sergeant nor the Duncans had spotted the rider.

Heck gestured toward the ridge, but when he turned back around, the rider had disappeared.

"We gotta make a run for it," he hollered back at the wagon and urged Red forward.

The big horse, his constant companion for the last decade, responded immediately and headed into the valley, across which Heck could just make out the strange formation of Petit Wells standing red and monolithic against the next ridge.

Looking back over his shoulder, he saw the rider come into view again… followed by a whole slew of warriors, all painted for war.

CHAPTER 12

"Stop the wagon," Heck hollered. He'd dropped back and was riding alongside Bruce Duncan, who continued to snap the reins, trundling along at the speed of certain death.

"Are you crazy?" Bruce said. "We can't stop now. Those are Indians!"

"Yes, they are," Heck said, "and if you don't stop now and double up with us, they are going to kill your family."

Bruce hesitated for only a second before halting the wagon.

The Indians were a few hundred yards away and closing fast.

"Ma'am," Sergeant Gentry said, giving Mabel Duncan a hand onto the back of his horse.

Clarence lifted Simon onto his.

Only Bruce Duncan hesitated. He turned and blinked at the wagon, which carried all his earthly possessions.

"But all of our things," Bruce said. "We can't—"

"Hold onto your rifle," Heck commanded then grabbed the man by his shirt and pulled him forward.

Bruce shouted with surprise and swung his leg over Red, and they charged away across the dusty land, chasing after the others, who raced at full speed toward the ring of red boulders some distance away.

Behind them, a rifle cracked. Then another.

Heck leaned over Red's neck, and the big horse, sturdy as always, pounded forward, overtaking the others and reaching Petit Wells first.

As Heck intended.

Not for his own safety but for that of Mabel Duncan and her son.

Because there just might be another party of Indians waiting inside.

Reaching the opening to the wells, he saw fresh tracks in the sandy ground.

"Hello the wells," he called.

A tall man with black hair, dark eyes, and a black goatee stepped into view. He held a rifle but did not aim it at Heck.

"Come in, come in," the man said, and there was authority in his voice, which, combined with his appearance and bearing, told Heck that he was some kind of misplaced gentleman.

European, by his accent.

The West was full of Europeans these days. Big game hunters, sightseers, businessmen, and fortune seekers.

Whatever the case, the man wasn't an Indian or a bandit. That's all that mattered now.

Heck rode forward as the others caught up.

Further back, the Indians had given up the chase and melted into the rocks.

Inside the ring of boulders waited a strange menagerie of folks. The dark-haired beauty with perfect posture, a long, straight nose, and several rings twinkling on her fingers could only be the gentleman's wife.

Standing beside her was a nervous-looking young woman with lots of honey-colored hair. Her pearl necklace and proximity to the dark-haired woman told Heck she was in some way related to the Europeans.

A short distance away, standing near the main pool, were two men in filthy army uniforms. The smaller of the pair cowered at his partner's side like a whipped dog.

The larger man wore a surly expression and regarded Heck with calculating eyes.

These two had to be Gentry's deserters. They appeared to be under arrest already, given their demeanor and the fact that their rifles leaned behind the women.

But if they were under arrest and the women were unarmed, who was guarding them? What was keeping them from running over and grabbing the guns?

"Howdy," a cheerful voice called from above, and Heck looked up to see a pleasant-looking kid a little younger than Seeker peering down from a perch among the boulders.

How, exactly, did the kid fit in? Was he with the Europeans? The girl's husband, perhaps, or brother?

"I don't get it," Bruce said. "Where are the Indians? They were chasing us. A bunch of them. But now they're gone. It makes no sense."

"Makes all the sense in the world," Heck said. "Sure, they

could have taken us, but at what cost? Once we reached the rocks, we would be fighting from cover, and they'd be out in the open. If they charged us, we'd slaughter most of them before they could break through. And the Sioux are far too intelligent to consider something like that a victory."

"Besides," Clarence said, "they didn't know how many other folks are in here."

"Is it over, then?" Mabel asked hopefully.

"No, ma'am," Heck said. "This isn't over. It's just beginning."

CHAPTER 13

B ruce Duncan went back out the passage to stand watch. The country was relatively open here, the Indians had stopped a good distance away, and the opposite side of the enclosure was flush against the next ridge, so one man could effectively stand guard.

For now, anyway.

The Sioux would take their time, using rocks, scrub, and darkness as cover while they moved inexorably closer, surrounding their position more and more tightly like a noose around a neck.

For now, however, Bruce could keep an eye.

A grim silence fell over the group. A silence that was broken when Sergeant Gentry, who had been studying the terrain and watching for Indians, finally rode forward and saw the two men standing near the pool.

"Privates Pipher and Twill, you men are under arrest!"

The smaller man cowered.

The big one stared back at Sergeant Gentry with murder in his eyes.

"You two cowards abandoned your post, leaving us open to attack," Sergeant Gentry said, dismounting and walking toward the deserters. "And because of your action, we *were* attacked. Attacked and wiped out with only one survivor—me."

"We didn't mean for nothing like that to happen, Sergeant," the smaller one yelped.

"Shut your mouth," Sergeant Gentry shouted. "I have every right to execute you both right now."

The big one surprised Heck by laughing. "You're telling me Barry and Hamlin are dead? That's the best news I've had all day. I hated those rotten sons of—"

Sergeant Gentry smashed the butt of his rifle into the big man's face, dropping him to the ground and opening a gash on one cheek. Then he backed up and shouldered the carbine.

"Go ahead and try it," Sergeant Gentry said. "Go ahead, Pipher, and I'll blow out your brains, what few you have. It's going to be a pleasure to watch you hang. And that's just what you'll do. Hang. At Fort Laramie. While everyone looks on, having heard exactly what you've done."

Pipher grinned up at the sergeant, touched the gash on his cheek, and examined the blood on his fingers. "I'll gut you for that, Gentry. If it's the last thing I do, I'll gut you like the big-mouthed carp you are."

"Don't talk like that, Hank," Twill said. "Sergeant Gentry, sir, I didn't mean for nothing like that to happen. I was just riding along with Pipher was all. To try and talk some sense into him. That was it. I was trying to—"

"Shut your lying mouth," Sergeant Gentry said, "or I'll bust your face too, Twill. Clarence, would you please give me a hand and tie up these men?"

"No offense, Sergeant Gentry," Clarence said, "but I got no fight with these men. My fight's with the Sioux."

"That's right, darky," Pipher snarled. "You stay out of it, or I'll gut you, too."

Clarence tilted his head a little. "You know, Sergeant Gentry, I guess maybe I will help you tie up these men, at least the one with the big mouth. Unless you'd rather I just shoot him instead."

"Gentlemen, please," the European said, stepping forward. "Now is not the time to allow old grievances to cloud our vision."

"Old grievances?" Sergeant Gentry protested. "I still have blisters from burying six good soldiers."

"I am terribly sorry for your loss," the European said, "but please, allow me to explain myself. These men, these deserters, clearly lack character. Why, even when my ladies and I rode into this place, they turned their guns on us."

Ladies? Heck thought, still trying to figure out who the blond-haired girl was to this Russian. Because that was what he was, Heck figured, based on his accent, some Russian nobleman or maybe a Russian military officer.

"We didn't know who you was," Twill whined. "That was all. We didn't do nothing to nobody."

"Shut up," Sergeant Gentry said, ready to lash out with his rifle butt.

"Gentlemen, please," the Russian said. "We cannot allow the heat to confuse us. I would ask you to hear me out, Sergeant, before proceeding. As I was saying, these men clearly lack character and just as clearly deserve punishment for their crimes. But it would be a mistake to bind them now."

"A mistake?" the boy said from up above, his voice lilting with incredulity. "They were gonna rob you and probably… well, I don't think they were gonna treat the women right."

"Yes," the Russian said, "and I thank you for coming to our aid, young man, but we must for a time forget these actions."

"Sounds like a good way to get killed," the kid said.

"The fact of the matter is," the Russian continued, "we need these men."

"They are the last two men on the face of the planet that we need," Sergeant Gentry declared. "Their cowardice resulted in the death of my soldiers."

"Wish they'd killed you, too, and saved me the trouble," Pipher sneered.

Sergeant Gentry lashed out with the butt of his rifle again, but this time, Pipher was ready for him.

The big man jerked his head to one side, slipping the blow, and was instantly on his feet.

Heck was surprised by the man's speed and agility.

Suddenly, Pipher had hold of Sergeant Gentry's rifle.

For a wild second, the two men wrestled for control of the weapon… until Clarence put the muzzle of his revolver against the back of Pipher's big head.

"Let go or die," Clarence said. "Your choice."

Apparently, the big deserter still wanted to live because he quit fighting and surrendered the rifle. "Now you made the list, too, darky."

"Gentlemen, please," the Russian said calmly. "Surely, you can forget your disagreements long enough to consider our present dilemma. We share a common enemy, the savages beyond the wall."

He paused, letting that sink in.

"I, for one, do not wish to die," the Russian continued. "Nor do I wish to see my ladies or any of you subjected to the wrath of the savages. For the time being, we must fight together. All of us must come together in defense of this position."

"Are you suggesting we arm these murderers?" Sergeant Gentry asked, squinting with disbelief.

"That is exactly what I am proposing," the Russian said coolly. "We need every rifleman, every guard we can muster. The savages are many. How else can we defend ourselves without their help?"

"Some help," Sergeant Gentry said. "You heard the man. He promised to kill me. You hand him a rifle, what's to stop him from blowing my head off?"

The Russian smiled. "Redemption."

"Redemption?"

"Yes, redemption. The only thing of real value to a condemned man. If Pipher and Twill do their duty and fight well, we let them go free."

"You're out of your mind," Sergeant Gentry said. "If you think I'm gonna—"

Suddenly, the Russian's pistol was in his hand and pointing straight at Sergeant Gentry.

CHAPTER 14

Heck was surprised at how quickly and smoothly he'd drawn and surprised, too, by how cool the Russian was in this tense moment. A gentleman he might be, but he was clearly more than just a gentleman.

He was also a fighting man. A practiced fighting man with poise and aptitude.

Heck respected that but drew his Colt just in case the air suddenly filled with lead.

The real enemy was outside. The Russian was right about that, anyway.

"Pardon my assertiveness," the Russian said, "but you must understand, my dear sergeant, that your duty is not the only thing at stake in this moment."

Sergeant Gentry glared at him.

The Russian said, "Also at stake are my life and the lives of my ladies, along with every life clustered here in this place. I cannot allow you to doom us. We must offer these men a reason to live in return for faithful service."

"I don't trust 'em," Clarence said. "I'm with Sergeant Gentry."

"They don't seem too trustworthy," the young man called down from his perch. "All that talk of gutting folks. I say we tie them up."

"My husband is right," the dark-haired woman said, and her accent was even more pronounced than his. "In moments such as these, we must set aside differences and pull together to face a common enemy. Let them fight the Indians. And then release them. Give them time to be on their way. Later, my good sergeant, if you wish to continue your hunt, that is between you and them. But here, in this place, we must stand together."

The blond-haired girl's eyes shone with admiration as she listened to the dark-haired woman's speech, much as they had when the husband had spoken. "I agree," she said, "I vote with Count Karpov."

It was the first time anyone had mentioned a vote, but Heck understood that was exactly what was happening here. They would each cast a vote to decide the thing—and all deal with the consequences, whatever they might be.

"I also vote to let them fight," Mabel Duncan said. "There are so many Indians. Why, I looked back, and it seemed the whole plain was painted for war. Let them fight, and if they serve honorably, well, forgiveness is chief among virtues."

"Ma'am," Sergeant Gentry said, "with all due respect, the soldiers I buried, they were good men. Christians, husbands, fathers. One was a grandfather. These men put their own families at risk to protect families like yours here on the frontier.

And now, they're dead because of these two remorseless deserters. No, ma'am, and no again, I will not forgive."

"I am truly sorry for your loss," Mabel Duncan said, sincerity thrumming in her voice, "but I stand with this man—Count... Kar...?"

"Count Viktor Karpov, ma'am," the tall Russian said with a practiced bow.

"I stand with Count Karpov," Mabel Duncan said. "And I'm certain my husband will as well."

Count Karpov smiled regally. "Which means the vote stands at five to three, Sergeant Gentry, if we count your vote, which does not seem entirely fair, unless we also count the votes of the condemned men."

"I vote for mercy!" the smaller man announced.

"Any further voting is inconsequential," Count Karpov said. "There are twelve people present. One is a child, two stand charged. That leaves nine. Five is a majority."

"I want to hear from the husband," Sergeant Gentry said. "Otherwise, she's getting two votes. He has to cast his own."

"Very well," Mabel Duncan said, moving toward the passage, "I will explain the situation and return with his vote."

Pipher grinned, his eyes flicking back and forth between the others.

There was something nasty about him, Heck decided, something cold and dangerous underneath all his bluster and threats. He reminded Heck of a reptile, a big, poisonous reptile that moved slowly—until it was time to strike, then moved with uncanny speed and deadliness.

"Mr. Duncan votes to let the men fight for their freedom," Mabel Duncan announced, returning to the group a short time later. "He says it's the Christian thing to do, as well as the wise thing, and a very American notion, giving these men a second chance at liberty."

Sergeant Gentry spat on the ground, mumbling, and turned away from the grinning Pipher. Gentry's knuckles went white as he squeezed the rifle. Then their color returned as they loosened their grip. His shoulders slumped in defeat.

"What about that tall fella yonder?" the boy on the ledge asked, nodding toward Heck. "He ain't cast a vote yet."

"An additional vote is unnecessary," the Count said with a winning smile. "The thing has been decided. Let us turn our attention to how, exactly, we will survive this situation."

"I vote for neither proposition," Heck said, ignoring the Count.

Confused faces regarded him.

"My friend," the Count said, "there is no other option. The choice is black or white. Condemnation or freedom. And these good people chose freedom."

"There is another choice," Heck said. "You want to free them. Sergeant Gentry wants to tie them up. I reckon we ought to just get it done with and shoot them."

There were a few gasps.

"Pipher, anyhow. He's rotten to the core. You can all see that. The man is a liability. I say we execute him straight away."

"That's barbaric," the blond-haired girl said.

"No, ma'am, it's not," Heck said. "It's the right thing to do. And the pragmatic thing as well. You mark my words, ma'am. If we allow Pipher to live, he will try to kill some of us before this is over. Why not finish him now and save the water he'll otherwise drink?"

Heck could see the notion hit home. Folks glanced past Pipher at the pool of dark water.

They had all known thirst these last few days. They all understood what awaited them if the water ran out.

"This debate is superfluous," Count Karpov said. "We handled the situation democratically. The majority voted for mercy and the common defense."

Heck grinned at him. He couldn't help it. This Russian was slick, and Heck didn't think for one second that the man cared a lick for the lives of Pipher and Twill. He just wanted the extra guns... and perhaps two more targets once the Indians started firing back.

Not that this man would be a coward. No, Heck could see the man had fighting spirit. Along with his composure and the way he handled the pistol, that made the Count a deadly man indeed.

"Oh no!" Bruce Duncan cried from down the passage. "They're burning the wagon!"

CHAPTER 15

The Russians, the blonde, and the Duncans hurried out the passageway to see the terrible sight.

Heck dismounted but did not join the others. He'd seen enough mayhem over the course of his life. Instead of watching the Duncans' world go up in flames, he figured he'd have a look around.

Pipher picked up his rifle and roared with laughter. "Thought you had us, huh, Gentry? Well, good old American democracy wins out in the end."

Sergeant Gentry shook his head, looking utterly defeated.

"Come on, Pete," Pipher said to Twill, strutting toward the passage. "Let's go watch the show. Not every day you get to watch a wagon burn."

As he swaggered past, Pipher cast a withering look in Heck's direction. "I won't forget what you said, buddy."

"What do you mean by that?"

Pipher stopped and glared at him. "I mean—"

"You're not threatening me, are you?" Heck said.

"What if I am?"

"Well, if you are threatening me, we have a problem. And if you and I have a problem, it won't be put to a vote. We'll settle it right here, right now. See, I don't take threats lightly. A man threatens me, says he's gonna kill me, there's only one logical response. I put him down."

As Heck said these words, he drilled a hard gaze into Pipher's eyes.

The burly man stared back but broke eye contact first and turned again to his sidekick. "Let's go before the whole thing burns up."

After they were gone, Clarence said, "I believe you just kicked the hornet's nest."

"Can't let Sergeant Gentry have all the fun, can we?" Heck laughed, clapping the dispirited sergeant on the shoulder. "Bide your time, my friend. The Count was right about one thing. We do need help."

"From the likes of these?" Sergeant Gentry said.

"Not for us to say. Folks voted against us. But we'll stick together. Pipher tries anything, you won't be alone."

"Much obliged, Heck."

Heck walked Red over to the main well, talking softly to the big stallion.

The pool was big and looked deep, but Heck knew that could be an illusion due to the dark water. These wells were mostly just catch basins for rain, which they hadn't seen for a mighty long time.

How much water did they actually hold? How long would it last twelve people and nine horses?

They would need to begin rationing water immediately, and they would need to be disciplined about that rationing.

Drinking more than one's allotted amount might very well result in the death of another. And with the Sioux certain to come for them, the death of any one of them might result in the death of all.

"I thought maybe you was gonna shoot him," the kid said from his perch.

"I would have if he'd lifted that rifle."

"And what if he doubled down on the threat?"

"I would've killed him."

The kid nodded, seeming to think about that. "Only way, I guess, a situation like that, a man like him."

"That's right. Only way. If you want to live."

"Well, I sure do want to live. I got plans out west. Gonna build me a stake, buy a farm, get a wife, raise some kids."

"Sounds like a good plan," Heck said. "You come here alone?"

The kid nodded. "I was with three others up until a few days ago, but the Indians hit us at the edge of the woods, and now, there's just me."

Heck thought about it for a second. "You got here before Pipher and his buddy?"

The kid nodded. "Hid up here until the Count and the women showed up. Pipher put the gun on them. I didn't like the way he was looking at the women, so I let him know I was up here and ready to pull the trigger."

Heck smiled. "Good man. My name's Heck Martin."

"Nice to meet you, Heck. I'm Cody Woodson."

"Can you see pretty good from up there?"

"Oh yeah. Farther up, I mean. You go up top, you can see the whole way around the circle pretty good."

"Any cover up there?"

"Yeah, not bad. Someone far off on top of that ridge yonder might be able to pick you off, but there's a rim that protects you from above and behind. That's the thing. They get up behind us, we're gonna have to step real careful."

Heck nodded. "I'm coming up for a look."

Heck slung his rifle over one shoulder and studied the rocks for a second. Bracing a foot against one boulder, he pushed his back against the other and slid upward.

Pressing with his elbow, he reached across, moved a foot up, and in this manner shimmied twenty feet to the ledge, where Cody gave him a hand.

"Good spot up here," Heck said, looking it over.

"Yeah, best spot I could find. I never dismounted down below. Climbed straight up out of the saddle."

Heck chuckled. "Smart. The Indians came here, found your horse, saw no fresh boot tracks, they might've thought the horse came on its own."

Cody grinned. "That's what I was hoping. And it worked with Pipher and Twill. Only real trouble here, if the Indians knew, would be ricochets. They shot enough bullets into these rocks, they would've got me sooner or later."

Heck nodded. "Later, probably. And not before you killed a bunch of them."

"That was the plan. But come on up. I'll show you the view from the top."

Heck followed him up the last ten feet to the broad, nearly flat top of the shorter boulder. Just as Cody had said, it was sheltered from above and behind by rimrock coming off the main ridge.

It was a good spot.

Out on the range, the Duncans' wagon burned, lifting a dark feather of smoke into the sky.

"That your wagon?" Cody asked.

"Nah. It belonged to the family. Their name's Duncan. Bruce, Mabel, and little Simon. The boy's a good kid. I sure do wish they hadn't drug him out here."

"Truth be told, I wish none of us was here," Cody said with a grin, "except maybe those two deserters."

"Amen to that."

"What are you doing out here, anyway? You seem like you know your way around. How did you get in this fix?"

Heck shook his head. "The Duncans came to my post." Briefly, he shared everything that had happened from that moment through his arrival here.

"Well, you did the right thing, anyway."

"Not if I get killed."

"How's that?"

"Because if I get killed, it won't matter that I was trying to help these folks. They'll be gone. All that'll matter will be that I left my own family in jeopardy."

Cody nodded, seeming to think about that for a moment. "Well then, Heck, I reckon you'd best not die."

Heck laughed, liking the kid. "Good plan, my friend. Good plan."

They stood there for a silent moment, looking out at the sunbaked land beyond their little oasis.

Heck swept his gaze slowly back and forth over the rocks

and ridges, sand and scrub.

Nothing moved.

Nothing, that is, save for the dancing flames engulfing the Duncans' wagon and the dark plume of smoke rising steadily into the bright and merciless sky.

But the Indians were out there, of course.

Heck hadn't seen them break off, but he figured they were two or three hundred yards out.

Or had been, anyway.

By this time, they would be working closer, moving with all the stealth and silence of a desert predator.

Which is exactly what they were. The unparalleled predators of the land.

And the Sioux loved situations like this, challenges like trying to move across a landscape with no obvious cover.

Yes, they were working closer. Or at least a few of them were.

They wouldn't attack unless they spotted an easy target.

Instead, they would watch and listen and wait.

No one could wait like an Indian. Patience and self-control were two of their greatest weapons.

They would use those weapons now to gather information. Once they knew more, they would make their plan. Then, at exactly the right moment, they would attack.

Normally, given the drought and the distance to the next well, the Sioux might attack suddenly.

But they had undoubtedly taken water barrels from the wagons. Indians and their ponies could live on very little water, so those barrels would buy them days, perhaps even weeks, before they needed to move.

Which meant their attack could come at any time. This instant. Or not for a week or longer.

Which gave them another weapon.

Tension.

The longer they delayed the attack, the more pressure would build among people here.

From down below came the sound of Mabel Duncan weeping.

It seemed a fitting song for the moment.

CHAPTER 16

Mabel Duncan couldn't seem to quit crying.

Even after the wagon had been reduced to a smoldering black lump in the distance, the sobs kept coming.

Yonder lay her whole life, all her hard work and saving, everything she had ever owned, burnt to ash.

Long after the others retreated into the wells, Mabel and her family remained at the mouth of the passage, staring out at the end of everything.

Little Simon clung to her leg, crying, which broke her heart, because the boy did not cry easily. He was only crying because she was crying.

"It's all right, son," she lied, rubbing his back. How she loved Simon. How she regretted bringing him here.

It was all so clear now.

And honestly, she supposed it should have been clear from the first moment that Bruce had come home, talking about the treasure map.

At that point, they hadn't had much, but they had been getting by, and more folks were moving into the region, planting crops, having babies, brightening things.

Mabel had been very happy.

Oh, they'd had a rough time of it a few years earlier—a terribly rough time, in fact—when the pox had struck, taking away her two oldest children, Bruce, Jr., and her flaxen-haired little angel, Felicity.

Thinking of her lost children made her cry all the harder. How she missed them. How she missed Junior's unruly hair and the way he followed Bruce everywhere, mimicking his every move.

And how she missed Felicity's laughter and the way the child found wonder and goodness in so many things. A born observer, little Felicity would pluck a seemingly ordinary blade of grass, bring it to Mabel, and point out all its amazing qualities, the thickness of the central vein or how one side was darker than the other or how the upper edge was slightly serrated if you only looked close enough.

See mother? See?

Mabel wept.

Oh, how happy they had been then.

Even after the pox, even after the unthinkable loss of her babies, they had managed to find their way back to happiness.

At least she had.

Bruce never spoke of the children, never admitted just how much he was hurting, but she knew he was. She would catch him sometimes, pausing at the doorway, half turning to wait for his little partner to follow him out and meet the day.

It was heartbreaking.

And of course, Simon would never take up that role. He was a hard little worker, but you had to tell him what to do, and he was more attuned to her than Bruce.

That's because he knows Mommy needs him, she thought, hugging the boy close.

Bruce stood there, staring out at the smoldering wagon with a look of shock and horror.

His eyes were dry, of course, but she knew he was hurting just as much as she was.

She wondered if he, too, was experiencing a heightened clarity of vision.

Did he see it all now? Did he understand that buying the map was foolish and that following it had been a fool's errand?

She'd questioned him—gently, of course—when he'd first raised the idea. But he had been adamant.

They were selling the farm, selling everything, and chasing this fortune.

She had wondered, briefly, if he was indeed hunting a bright future—or simply running away from a dark past.

Whatever the case, they were ruined now, just as, looking back, she should have known they would be ruined when he came through the door smiling as if everything was well in the world.

She choked bitterly, remembering her thought at that moment, that something wonderful must have happened, because it was the first time she had seen him really smile since they'd lost the children.

But oh, how wrong she had been. That smile had been poison. Pure poison.

She had not argued, of course. She was a good wife, and that meant obeying her husband, having faith in him, and supporting him in any way she could.

So she did not merely hold her tongue. She took these things to heart and kindled a small fire of optimism.

Several times along the way, the fire nearly went out.

Most notably, when they reached Hope City, and Heck Martin tried to talk them out of the trip.

He was right, of course. He was right about everything.

And she'd known that, standing there across the counter from him, just as she had known he was right every time he and Bruce had disagreed along the way.

Heck Martin understood this country.

She and Bruce did not. They were farmers. And that was fine. She had been happy as a farmer.

This, however…

How would they ever recover from this?

Everything was gone. Even the cursed map.

She felt a tug at her sleeve and looked down to see Simon staring up at her with a compassionate expression. "Are you okay, Mommy?"

"Yes, sweet child," she said, lying again—but what mother wouldn't lie at such a moment? "Yes, it was a bit of a shock, but I'm all right."

"Good. I was worried about you."

She leaned and took him under the arms and lifted him into an embrace. "Oh, don't you worry about Mommy, sweet Simon," she cooed, rubbing his back. "I'm all right. Everything is going to be all right."

She was surprised to realize she was gaining strength from comforting her frightened son.

Which made sense, of course.

Wallowing in self-pity never helps anyone. It's unavoidable sometimes, but self-pity always weakens, never strengthens.

The thing to do, she resolved, breathing deeply and rubbing her son's back, was to stay strong. First, for Simon, then for herself.

And, of course, for Bruce, who still stared blankly out into the distance as if something inside him had burned along with their wagon.

She would have to do what she could for him. But first, Simon.

She rocked the boy, humming gently to him the way she had when he was very small.

"Mommy?"

"Yes, love?"

"I want to go home."

Home is gone, she thought. *We have no home.*

But what she said was, "We will, Simon."

"Can we go now? I don't like this place."

"No, I'm afraid we can't leave just yet. But we will when we can."

"Mr. Martin could get us home."

"Yes," she said and looked again to her husband, not wanting to wound his pride but needing to give her son hope. "Yes, I believe Mr. Martin will get us home, Simon."

And just like that, she knew she believed those words. If anyone could get them out of this horrible nightmare, it was Heck Martin.

Bruce's eyes remained unfocused.

That was problematic. He had volunteered, after all, to stand watch.

What if, while he stared blankly, the Indians had been sneaking closer?

She scanned the dusty bowl before her and to each side but saw nothing.

Wait... had that been movement to the left, two hundred yards away?

She stared hard. Nothing was moving now.

Glancing at her husband, she saw he was still gazing deep into nothingness.

She considered speaking to him, jarring him out of his malaise, but decided against it. Doing so would add embarrassment to his obvious pain.

She could better support him by allowing this temporary weakness and standing in silently for him, keeping watch herself.

"Mommy, are we really going to be okay?" Simon asked.

"Yes, dear," Mabel said, and kept raking her gaze across the rugged landscape. "We are going to be all right. I promise to take care of you."

With the promise, Mabel let that truth sink in.

She never should have put her faith in Bruce.

He was a good man and worthy of faith in so many ways. Being a loving and caring husband and father; working hard, regardless of conditions, and keeping food on the table; knowing the best course of action when weather or pests threatened a crop...

But not here. Not this.

Here, she could only rely on Heck Martin. And, she was coming to realize, herself.

Yes, that more than anything.

She had to get tough, had to rely on herself.

CHAPTER 17

Count Viktor Karpov lingered near the pool, pretending to examine his horse, until he and his women were alone. Then, he unfastened the lockbox from his horse and told Natalia and Becky, "Stand here. If anyone comes, talk to them."

"About what?" Becky asked.

"Anything. It does not matter. But you must occupy them while I hide the lockbox. I do not trust these people. And if anyone knew about the gems and jewelry, we would be in grave danger."

"Of course, my dear husband," Natalia said. "Go hide the box. We will stand watch."

With the box tucked beneath one arm, Viktor went under the rimrock, circled the main pool, and stayed close to the back wall, looking for a proper hiding place.

The air was cool and still beneath the rimrock. He passed two other pools, both smaller than the main well, and focused on the back wall.

It was important to disguise the box, but he also wanted to be able to retrieve it quickly in case they left in a hurry.

Finding a small depression at the base of the wall, he pushed the box inside and covered it over with stones, then stood back and took a look.

Good.

When he returned to the main pool, the women were talking to the loathsome Hank Pipher.

"Gentry only told one part of the story," Pipher said. He looked Natalia and Becky up and down, undressing them with his eyes. "*His* part. There's a lot more to it than that. Trust me.

Gentry's a liar."

The women fidgeted, clearly uncomfortable with his attention.

Seeing Viktor approaching, Pipher grinned and held out a big hand. "There he is."

Viktor shook the hand, hiding his distaste.

Pipher's hand was huge and hard with callouses, like the hand of a troll.

"Hey, Count, thanks for sticking up for us back there. I won't forget it." Pipher turned a slimy smile on the women. "I take real good care of my friends."

"Nothing less than I would expect," Viktor said. "Justice was done. Whatever occurred between you and the army has nothing to do with this situation. Here, we must remain unified. And now, the road to redemption lies wide open to you and Mr. Twill. I know you will pass through its gates and into better lives."

Viktor knew nothing of the sort, obviously, but he wanted

to underscore Pipher's end of the deal. The big soldier had to serve well and fight well.

Pipher guaranteed he would do just that, then drifted away across the enclosure.

Viktor was pleased. He had hidden the box and gently echoed his expectations with Pipher.

Everything was coming together.

As a Russian nobleman, he could not help but view the situation in terms of chess.

This was still the opening portion of the game.

Beyond the enclosure, the savages were no doubt moving to more advantageous positions and preparing a plan.

Meanwhile, he was moving his own pieces into position. Mostly, that meant manipulating these people, these pawns, to best protect him, his women, and his possessions.

Once the Indians were satisfied with their arrangement, they would attack, initiating the middle game with all its attacks and sacrifices, when the loss of material might set up a winning endgame.

That, of course, was everything.

Setting up the endgame that won it all.

But the opening wasn't merely getting your pieces to their proper squares. It also required analysis and planning and a constant eye toward subtle dangers.

Here, in this waterless land, the ultimate danger was thirst.

To endure the fight and what would come after, they needed to think of thirst. Now, while the others still believed the water supply was more than sufficient.

"Drink deep, ladies," Viktor told Natalia and Becky. "And keep your canteens full. When we make our break, there will be no water for many miles. We, our canteens, and our animals must be full of water."

"Which would make a lot of sense if you three were alone," a deep voice said behind him.

He turned and saw the tall man, the one who had proposed they execute Pipher, standing thirty or forty feet away.

Viktor had spoken softly to the women. How had this man even heard his words?

"Trouble is, there's a dozen of us and nine horses, not just you and yours. That water won't last forever."

"We don't need the water to last forever," Viktor said. "We only need it to last until we've beaten the savages."

"And when do you plan to do that?"

"As soon as they attack, of course," Viktor said, exaggerating his confidence in their position. "We will be firing from cover. There's no place to hide out there."

The man laughed humorlessly. "Mister, I've seen Sioux warriors hide where no man had business hiding. Scrubby ground like that out there, well, they'll get as close as they want before they choose to attack. If they choose to attack."

"If?" Natalia asked. "Do you believe the savages will leave us alone?"

"Leave us alone?" The man offered an irritating smile. "No, ma'am. Not hardly. Not with you ladies and these horses inside. They will not leave all that. But they might decide not to attack and wait us out instead."

"A ridiculous notion," Viktor said. He was aware of others gathering closer and listening, and he resented this man questioning him this way. "Petit Wells holds the only water for miles and miles. If anyone is able to wait the other out, it is us."

The tall man shook his head. "They got water from wagon barrels, remember? Plus whatever they were packing. Besides, an Indian can live on far less water than we can. And he knows enough to ration what he's got."

This last comment, an obvious jab, annoyed Viktor. "You sound, sir, as if you admire these savages."

"Admire them? Not exactly. Though they do possess numerous admirable traits, along with some downright harrowing ones. I respect them. See, I know Indians. I've fought them, but I've also traded with them and ate in their tents and smoked their peace pipes. I've negotiated treaties with them and went to war when those treaties fell apart. I've hunted with them and been hunted by them. So I understand and respect them and yes, in some ways, even admire them."

Most of the people were gathered around now, listening intently to the tall man, who went on.

"They will likely attack. Not all at once. It would make more sense for them to wait and wear us down. Shoot anyone who gets careless and makes himself a target. Maybe run a few probing raids. And yes, they might even venture an all-out assault. If so, I'd expect it to come around dawn."

"Tomorrow?" someone asked.

"Tomorrow, the next day, a week or two," the tall man said, spreading his hands in a surprising display of showmanship Viktor wouldn't have expected from a filthy frontiersman.

But the man was clearly used to being heard and had probably even led men before, given the way he spoke and gestured.

"The one thing you can count on is unpredictability," the tall man said. "They will attack how and when it best suits them.

And yes, they might simply draw back and wait for us to crack. That's what I would do."

He pointed to the pool and raised his voice, speaking not to Viktor but to everyone. "We must ration this water. It won't last forever. And if it runs out, we're finished."

CHAPTER 18

Hank Pipher stepped away from the group, feeling surly.

It wasn't that he disagreed with what the tall fella had said. In fact, it was smart, thinking about water now, while they still had plenty.

Pipher just didn't like being told what to do. That was all. And he didn't like the tall man, either.

Because the man liked to play boss. That much was obvious.

Like talking about rationing water or suggesting they execute Pipher.

Man practically had a God complex.

Well, Pipher wouldn't forget what he'd tried to do. Man like that, calling for execution, putting no value on life, why, he was a danger to everyone.

Sooner or later, Pipher would get his chance, though, and eliminate that danger.

If it came down to it, he could always push the man a little, let him talk tough again, then take him up on it.

Pipher had always been quick with his fists or a gun. He would gun down the tall man before the know-it-all even got his hammer back.

But folks wouldn't like that, and Gentry would crow about it, call for justice, all that nonsense.

That wouldn't be good. He didn't want to kill the tall man yet, anyway. Not while the Injuns were still out there, laying for them.

Pipher didn't necessarily believe all the tall man's talk about Injuns, smoking peace pipes and eating in their tents and all that, but he did look like he'd been around, so he'd probably be a good man to have on your side when the attack came.

But yeah, eventually, once there weren't so many Injuns, Pipher would get him.

The best way to do it would be to wait for another Indian attack, then shoot the tall man in the back.

Yeah. That's what he would do.

Stuff like that happened all the time in combat.

Pipher should know. He'd done it himself. More than once.

But that was for later.

Right now, he had bigger fish to fry, anyway.

The Count's fish, to be precise. The women and whatever he had in that box of his.

He'd hidden the box somewhere by the other pools.

Pipher hadn't seen him carry it off, let alone hide it, but he had noticed the box, and then it was gone, and when Pipher was talking to the women, the Count had come walking back out with no box in sight.

So it stood to reason he'd hidden it back there.

What was in that box?

Why would the Count, a man who apparently had hired teamsters to drive three wagonloads of stuff, feel the need to carry a lone box on his own horse—then to hide it away from everyone?

Must be something really valuable in there.

Gold, Pipher reckoned. And lots of it.

Some folks, you could tell they had money just by the way they looked. Not even their clothes and such. You could tell by their faces and the way they stood and talked.

This count was like that. The way he carried himself, the way he talked, the way he looked… the man had money.

Besides, he had two women, didn't he?

How could he get two women, especially two fine-looking women, without a whole bunch of money?

Well, one thing was certain. Pipher was gonna take a look inside that box.

Then, when the moment was right, if the box turned out to be holding the sort of thing he expected, he would be ready to snatch it and run.

He couldn't grab it yet. Where would he take it?

The Injuns out there were just waiting for somebody to break and run for it.

So no, he wouldn't take the box yet. But the first chance he got, he was gonna go back there and take a look.

He couldn't let anybody see him, especially the Count.

Pipher grinned suddenly, because he knew exactly how he was gonna get to the box.

"Pipher," a deep voice called from behind him.

He turned, and it was the tall man.

"Your turn to stand watch," the tall man said.

"Says who?"

"Says me."

"I don't see no roster."

"We don't have one yet. But it's time to relieve Bruce and Cody. I figured I'd relieve Cody. Unless you'd rather crawl up those boulders and have me take the front guard."

Pipher glanced at the boulders and the long climb up smooth rock to the ledge. He could do it, but it wouldn't be fun, and besides, he didn't want to be trapped all by himself like that, with no place to run. He didn't trust these people.

"That's all right, boss," Pipher said. "I'm just messing with you is all. You climb up and take over for the kid. I'll relieve Bruce. Put in some redeeming work, right? Earn my pardon, since they voted you down when you wanted to kill me?"

"My suggestion made sense, given the fact that you were threatening to kill Sergeant Gentry."

"And the darky. Don't forget him. But hey, I was just talking was all, blowing hot air. You don't have to worry about me. I'm gentle as a lamb."

CHAPTER 19

C ount Viktor Karpov examined the enclosure carefully, walking its perimeter and checking for any hidden weakness.

Know the terrain, the General always told him. *It is a weapon. It will be used by you or against you.*

Viktor found no secret weakness in their position. They were vulnerable from above, of course, if the savages managed to reach the ridge behind them, but the cliff was sheer, and firing with accuracy from the top would be difficult. Meanwhile, down here on the ground, there was one way in, the easily guarded passage at the front.

Even if the Indians were to fire down from above, he could retreat beneath the rim and be safe. And that's where the water was.

So this was a viable position against this force, which he judged to be around two dozen savages.

Meanwhile, they had eight men, three women, and a child.

He had learned from his father that a fighting force defending a strong position could hold off three times as many attackers.

Eight men. Eight times three was twenty-four.

Almost exactly the number they would face.

So, a deadlock.

Unless the women would fight.

Natalia would fight in a pinch. She was not trained, but she possessed inner strength.

Would Becky fight?

He couldn't imagine her firing a weapon and didn't like to try. Somehow, the notion tainted her.

She came from the dirt, of course, working fields and tending children and animals, but he had rescued her from that existence and given her nice clothes and the necklace.

To interrupt that tale would somehow lessen her. He wanted to preserve his peasant maiden.

And Mrs. Duncan?

The last he'd seen her she'd been sobbing uncontrollably, but that was understandable enough. She was watching her wagon burn and coming to terms with her situation.

He suspected once the moment passed that she would prove to be a sturdy woman. She seemed sensible enough, and he'd heard many frontier women were familiar with firearms.

If one or two women would stand and fight, that might provide the crucial mathematical edge.

But was that even possible? How many rifles did they have?

His extra rifles were lost. Worse than lost, he realized suddenly. They were in the hands of the savages, along with most of his shot and powder and everything else.

The thought of being killed by weapons he had purchased and packed into this godforsaken place irked him.

Well, he would not let that happen.

Was there a way to bargain with the savages?

He'd heard tales of men buying vast tracts of land or stacks of beaver pelts with a handful of glass beads. But something told him that would not be possible with these savages.

They didn't want beads. They wanted blood.

Not to mention the horses and the women.

Well, he would not trade his horses and strand himself here. Perhaps he could persuade some of the others to trade theirs?

Doubtful.

And what of the women?

No. He would trade neither Natalia nor Becky, especially not when the odds were even.

He wanted both women.

What of Mrs. Duncan?

Unfortunately, Mr. Duncan would never let her go, especially not with a son present.

But if Mr. Duncan died...

No, that would only weaken their position. The loss of any man now would tilt the balance in favor of the savages.

So, with no way to bargain, they must fight. Which suited Viktor. He loved combat, and he had been wanting to slaughter some of these famous savages.

His thoughts returned to the available firearms.

Natalia carried a derringer.

Each of the men had at least one rifle. But how much shot and powder did they have?

His own supply was lower than he would have liked. Twenty

balls for the Enfield, six rounds for the Navy Colt, and a quarter pound of powder.

He would have to make every shot count.

Would the other men fight wisely?

Sergeant Gentry was clearly experienced but was also ragged and distracted by his conflict with the deserters.

That had been a smart move on Viktor's part, lobbying for the deserters' freedom.

They didn't deserve mercy, of course. They were vile men, coarse and dishonorable, but he needed them. For now, every defender was crucial.

But they were the sort to crack under pressure. Especially Pipher. He was the type of man who would always have a problem, always savor a grudge.

For men like Pipher, life was a constant fight. And if they weren't clashing with someone, they started looking for trouble, even creating it, because they didn't know how to live without dispute.

Sooner or later, Pipher would pick a fight within the group. A real fight, a fight to the death. Because in a place such as this, real fights could only end in death.

So yes, it had been a wise move on Viktor's part to suggest pardoning the man. Because that made it less likely that Pipher would set his sights on Viktor.

Not that Viktor feared him. He feared no man. And he had bested far better men than Pipher.

But Pipher lacked honor. He might attack an opponent in his sleep, without warning, or shoot an adversary in the back.

Men like that made bad enemies but valuable assets.

And what of the others?

The fellow with Pipher, Pete Twill, reminded Viktor of a nervous lap dog. He was attached to Pipher, probably because he feared him, and would do what the big man said unless his underlying cowardice prevented obedience.

Bruce Duncan was a farmer, but what of it? The Russian ranks were full of farmers.

Duncan seemed comfortable with his rifle and had probably done a fair amount of hunting. He would fight to protect his family and didn't seem like the type to cause trouble. He would do.

And the Black man, Clarence?

He was quiet but decisive, which he proved when he put the gun to Pipher's head. He looked like an experienced frontiersman. He would stand.

The boy from the ledge seemed calm enough, too, and he had already proven himself to some degree, coming to Viktor's aid when the deserters were planning to rob him and have their way with his women.

Though, speaking of the women, Viktor did not like the way the boy looked at Becky. He did not ogle her the way some men did, but Viktor noticed the boy—Cody was his name, he remembered—noticed Cody sneaking glances every time Becky looked away.

Well, perhaps Viktor could use that to his advantage. Perhaps the boy would fight all the harder to protect and impress Becky.

If Viktor allowed Cody to talk with Becky, the boy might go to heroic lengths to protect her and, by extension, all of them. But what if Becky became interested in the boy?

Viktor smiled at the thought, amused by his own posses-siveness.

There was no chance of that happening, of course. Becky was traveling with nobility, and she clearly recognized Viktor's character, class, and strength.

By contrast, the boy would doubtlessly seem common and footloose, like a clod of dirt from the life she had escaped that had somehow followed her here to this place, this brief and inconvenient stop on the way to her sparkling new life in California.

So yes, he would allow her to speak with Cody if the boy tried.

Finally, there was the tall man—Viktor had heard someone call him Heck, a ridiculous name for a ridiculously tall brute.

Heck was clearly a fool. Why else, when the matter was already decided, would he propose executing Pipher?

Didn't he know that such a proposal would put him directly in Pipher's sights?

Still, this Heck seemed like a hard, confident man. He looked stupid with his fringed buckskin clothing, but his blue eyes gleamed with something like intelligence. Probably the cunning of a predator.

Yes, he was likely a dangerous man. And that was good. Viktor needed dangerous, capable men to defend him now.

So long as Heck did not become a liability. If he proved himself to be a competent warrior then questioned Viktor's rule, as he had near the pool, he might undermine Viktor's authority among commoners such as these, especially when they feared for their lives.

He remembered how confidently Heck had spoken when

proposing the execution of Pipher and again, by the pool, when he had spoken of rationing water.

Viktor also remembered how everyone had looked at Heck then, giving him their full attention.

So yes, Heck was a valuable defender but potentially dangerous to Viktor's authority.

And Viktor could not allow Heck to undermine his authority.

Under different circumstances, he would deal with this man as he had so many others. Wait for a moment to pretend offense, then propose a duel, kill him, and move on.

But that wasn't possible here. Or at least not advisable. Because seven times three was only twenty-one.

So no. He would not kill Heck.

Then he had it.

He would not engineer some offense to justify a duel. Instead, he would engineer an official vote.

Just as he had initiated a vote concerning Pipher, he would initiate a vote concerning leadership. In a situation such as this, a military situation, leadership was necessary.

And clearly, Viktor was the man for the job.

Presently, he had the confidence of the majority.

All he needed was a vote. It wouldn't do for *him* to propose the vote, of course.

Perhaps he would have Natalia or Becky propose a vote and nominate him, though it would be even better if someone outside his group suggested the vote. Then Natalia or Becky could nominate Viktor.

Yes, that was the way.

But how could he convince someone to do that?

Through the women. He would use Natalia or Becky. Have one of them quietly suggest the idea to another. Then nominate Viktor and hold the vote before increased fear magnified the power of Heck's surly confidence.

Yes, that was what he would do.

CHAPTER 20

"Any movement out there?" Heck asked, joining Clarence at the top of the rock.

"Nothing I can see. But the Sioux are crafty."

"Yes, they are. I don't reckon they're in any hurry, though. They can get as close as they want come nighttime."

Clarence nodded, still staring out into the sun-bleached scrubland. "Of course, they know we're thinking that way. Might even think we aren't expecting an attack now, which would make us vulnerable."

"I can see you're a man with a healthy respect for his enemy."

"That I am. I've found that having respect for my enemies helps to keep me from getting killed."

Heck grinned. "I've noticed the same thing. Speaking of enemies, I figure sooner or later Pipher will try something."

"Oh yeah. He'll try something. You notice he moves kind of quick for a man that size?"

"I did notice that. Smooth, too. Kind of jarring, what with him being so big and bullheaded, but the man moves with speed and grace."

"Deadly combination."

"Yes, sir, it is," Heck agreed. "I thought maybe I'd draw him out, but he didn't take the bait."

"You sure you can beat him?"

"I can beat him. If it's a standup fight. But something tells me he doesn't live by the code duello."

"No. I reckon he's more likely to shoot one of us in the back when the Sioux make their move."

"Could be. But we might be giving him too much credit. He might be a blowhard."

"Maybe. But I won't stake my life on it."

"Neither will I. But we've only known Pipher for a few hours, and he's already threatened to kill a few people. Man like that is either a blowhard or has a stack of bodies in his back trail. If he killed a bunch of folks, seems like Sergeant Gentry would know."

"That's a good point. But I'm still not letting my guard down."

"You'd be a fool if you did."

"Well, my mama didn't raise no dummies. I'll just keep one eye open when I sleep."

"What do you say we keep an eye out for each other, too?"

"Sounds good, Heck." Clarence stuck out his hand.

Heck shook it. "Deal, then. I'll watch your back. You watch mine."

"I suppose Gentry will keep an eye, too."

"And Cody seems all right."

"That the kid who was hiding up here?"

Heck nodded. "I talked to him a little. He's young, but he seems capable."

"I don't like this situation one bit. Think we could ride out at night?"

Heck shook his head. "I reckon they'd get us out in the open. You know they're watching. And where would we go? The water's here. Next well is far off."

"Twenty-seven miles."

"Long way. Besides, we don't have enough horses, not for that kind of riding. We could double up for a short distance like we did, racing here, but sooner or later under these conditions that would kill the horses. No, we gotta sit this out."

"Well, I'm gonna go see to my horse. He doesn't know me well. Took him off some bandits who tried to kill me a few days back."

Clarence told Heck about the bandits ambushing him and how he'd evaded and eventually killed them with the help of a hungry buzzard.

"That was good thinking," Heck said.

"Gotta keep thinking if you want to survive in country like this," Clarence said. "And you need a strong bond with your horse, too. Which is why I gotta go see mine. Gonna treat him right, show him what kind of man I am."

Clarence left, and Heck took up his watch.

It was hot, even hotter than down below, but at least the rim blocked the sun.

That wouldn't be the case in the morning. The position faced east, so it would heat up early, and seeing would be harder.

Maybe even much harder, especially on a clear day.

Would the Sioux know that?

Yes.

They would know the well, all its ins and outs, including Cody's bench and this spot.

And even if they didn't know this place, they would know the passage faced east.

So they were more likely to attack in the morning than in the afternoon.

Or would they come at night?

Perhaps.

Some tribes avoided night fighting for superstitious reasons, but he'd never heard that about the Sioux.

And among the Sioux, of course, every tribe had their own ways, so they would just have to see.

He remembered the foolish raid young braves from a different group, the Bone Canyon Sioux, had staged on Heck's Valley back before there were many people living there.

The Bone Canyon Sioux had counted on even fewer. And they'd died for that oversight, charging straight into an ambush by Heck and friends, who'd positioned themselves on either side of the valley and cut them to ribbons.

He wished he had those friends with him now. With a force that size, they could fight their way out of here.

The help of friends was something to hope for if the siege stretched on for a long time, which it very well might.

If Seeker came home from visiting his uncle in the mountains and heard Heck was still on the trail, he would muster a party and ride out. Guaranteed.

But Heck had no idea when Seeker would be coming home.

It might not be for weeks, or he could be riding this way even now with a bunch of volunteers.

The Mullen men would come, of course. Paul Wolfe would come, too; he'd turned into quite a fighter since that first skirmish several years ago. Doc Skiff and Ray McLean, Burt Bickle and Dusty Maguire, Abe Zale and Shorty Potter and a slew of others would insist on coming along.

Which presented a new problem.

He didn't want his friends riding into trouble.

If Seeker was with them, they'd be all right. He'd be cautious and read the signs.

But what if the others got anxious and left without Seeker?

It was something to consider.

How could he warn them so they didn't ride straight into an ambush?

It was something to think about.

A lone buzzard materialized on the horizon, circling over the spot where the Count must have lost his wagons and his hired men.

Heck wondered briefly if it might be Clarence's buzzard then turned his thoughts to what they must do.

At least two people needed to stand watch at all times, one in the passage, one up here.

From this elevated post, a guard wouldn't be able to see much at nighttime. Even if there was a sliver of moon overhead, the Sioux could move like ghosts in moonlight.

The advantage to keeping a guard up here even at night was the watcher's ability to see or hear any movement atop the boulders. If warriors crawled in close and tried to come over the top, the watcher here would spot them and sound the alarm.

So yes, they needed to keep a guard here at night, too.

Everyone would need to pitch in, providing rest for the others.

He knew some would bellyache.

They would also complain when he suggested pooling resources.

He had a fair amount of pemmican in his bags and a good deal of shot and powder.

What about the others?

Most were probably running thin on food.

The Count, like the Duncans, had lost everything when the Sioux had taken their wagons.

But the Count also had saddle bags, as did his female friends, and he had that big box lashed to his horse.

What was he carrying in there?

Hopefully food, but Heck doubted it.

The box had a lock, after all, so it more likely held money than food.

Whatever the case, Heck would suggest inventorying, sharing, and rationing supplies.

The Count wouldn't like that. He had certainly been angry when Heck had suggested going easy on the water.

Some men didn't like to be told what to do. But in a situation like this, everyone had to work together to survive.

So yes, they should pool resources. That would help them understand their situation, how much food they had, how much ammo, how much time.

This, in turn, would define limitations, which would present choices.

And they couldn't form a plan without understanding their choices.

Something flashed out in the valley, perhaps two hundred yards away, sun on steel. A rifle cracked, and down below, Pipher cursed loudly.

Heck lifted his rifle, hoping to return fire, but the shooter was long gone.

The world was silent again—save for Pipher bellowing about how close the bullet had come—and absolutely still, as if there had been no sniper, no gunshot, no near miss.

Heck took a measured sip from his canteen.

This was setting up to be a long, brutal fight. And Heck was beginning to suspect not all enemies were on the other side of the boulders.

CHAPTER 21

Cody was sitting under the rim near the pool, cleaning his rifle and chewing on a hunk of jerky, when a soft voice said, "Excuse me, sir?"

He looked up and almost choked. It was the blond-haired girl.

She sure was pretty. More than pretty, actually. She was gorgeous, the most beautiful girl he'd ever seen.

He'd thought she was older, like twenty or twenty-one, but up close, he could see she was probably around his age, and certainly no older than eighteen.

"Yeah?" he said then remembered his manners and stood up, took off his hat, and struggled against the temptation to start dusting off his duds. "I mean, yes, ma'am?"

His face burned, and he knew he was blushing. He'd never been any good at talking to girls. He'd never had much practice, after all. They made him nervous. Especially pretty ones around his age.

"I just wanted to say thank you." She smiled at him, and his face burned all the hotter.

"Thank you?"

"Yes, for what you did."

"What I did?" As soon as the words were out of his mouth, he knew what she'd meant, but he was so overcome by her nearness that it seemed all he could do was repeat whatever she said and make an even bigger fool out of himself.

"Yes, standing up for us when Pipher and Twill threatened the Count."

"Oh, that. Well, that was nothing, ma'am."

"Nothing? It was brave. And smart, too. Did you really hide up there for days?"

Cody nodded. Her calling him brave and smart made him feel better, giving him a little confidence, but he hastened to set her straight.

"That wasn't brave, ma'am. I had the drop on them."

She smiled. "Well, I think it was terribly brave."

She extended her hand. "My name is Rebecca Bonneville, but I hope you'll call me Becky. All my friends do."

Cody took her hand and panicked a little at the warm reality of it. He was touching her, touching the most beautiful girl he'd ever seen!

But what was he supposed to do? Shake her hand? Kiss it?

Afraid to make a mistake, he just stood there staring at her until she started pumping his hand up and down, then released it and tilted her head a little, smiling curiously. "Are you all right?"

"Yes, ma'am. I'm fine."

"Do you want me to leave you alone?"

"No, ma'am. Please don't go. I mean, unless you want to."

She laughed. It was a beautiful sound. "Where would I possibly go?"

He laughed nervously, hating the sound of it.

"Well, my brave savior, are you going to be a good sport and tell me your name, too?"

Cody felt like slapping himself in the forehead. What was wrong with him? She'd introduced herself, and he just stood there, gawking at her, like he was still doing now...

"Cody," he blurted. "My name's Cody."

"All right, Cody. It's nice to meet you. Do you have a last name?"

"Yes, ma'am. It's Woodson. Cody Woodson."

"Well, thank you again, Cody. I hate to think what would have happened if you hadn't been there. The Count is a very strong man, but there were two of them, and I don't think they are very nice."

"No, ma'am, they're not."

Remembering the moment, how those two thugs had melted before him, Cody wiped the rag lovingly across his barrel.

"I'll let you get back to cleaning your gun," Becky said.

"No," Cody said quickly. "I mean, that's all right, ma'am. It's not even dirty. Not really. I just clean it every day is all. Inside and out."

"Even if you don't shoot it?"

"Yes, ma'am."

"My name is Becky, remember? You call me ma'am, it makes me sound like an old lady."

"Sorry, Becky."

"That's all right, Cody. How come you clean your rifle so much?"

"I take care of my things. My rifle, my horse, my boots. I never really had much, but what I do have, I take care of."

Becky smiled for some reason and then opened her mouth, like she was fixing to say something, but seemed to think better of it and left the thing unsaid.

An awkward silence followed. Cody struggled, trying and failing to think of something to say.

"Count Karpov is very wealthy," Becky said.

"Oh yeah? What's he doing out here, then?"

"We're on our way to California."

"Are you… related to him?"

Becky shook her head, bringing her blond curls to life. "He's my benefactor."

"What's that mean?"

"Like my employer. I'm his traveling companion."

He felt a wave of relief. So, the Count was her boss, not her husband.

"He gave me this," she said with a big smile and lifted the necklace from her throat. "It's a pearl necklace. It's worth an awful lot of money. Not that I'd ever sell it, of course. But still. Wasn't that nice of him?"

"Sure was," Cody said, but something about this whole setup wasn't quite level. "What kind of work do you have to do, being a traveling companion?"

"Work?" Becky laughed. "A traveling companion doesn't work. I just accompany the Count and Countess. That's all."

Cody nodded and with his tongue traced a slow circle around the inside of his cheek.

He didn't know much about women, but he'd heard stories of a type of girl who made their living...

No. A sweet girl like Becky couldn't do that.

Could she?

He didn't want to believe, didn't even want to consider the possibility.

But why else would the Count give her something worth hundreds or maybe even thousands of dollars just to travel with him?

Unless that necklace was an investment, and he had plans for her down the trail, after he got her far away from her kin.

It was a nasty thought. But better than the other. At least it preserved Cody's notion of her, the way he'd like to think of her.

"The Count isn't just wealthy," Becky said. "He's very strong and experienced. He should be our leader."

"Our leader?"

"Sure. Don't you think? There's been an awful lot of squabbling. We need a strong leader to unite us."

"How would you get them to all agree on a leader?"

"With a vote, of course. An official vote. I would propose it, but since I'm with the Count, it might not seem as proper for me to suggest it, not like if someone else proposed a vote."

"I see what you mean."

Becky smiled again. She sure was pretty. "Hey, you know what? That gives me an idea, Cody."

CHAPTER 22

The setting sun tinged the world in hues of fire and blood, pitching long shadows from tufts of tinder-dry grass.

The heat of day lingered on, though Heck knew the temperature would plummet with nightfall. In a bowl like this with a clear sky overhead, the night would be cold and full of stars.

What else would night bring?

An attack?

There was no way to tell.

They would just have to wait—and not be broken by the waiting.

Meanwhile, Heck crouched beside the main pool and frowned at the water line, which had already dropped noticeably.

He broke off a mesquite branch and moved around the pool, dipping the stick into the water several times.

His frown deepened.

Just as he had suspected, the pool was nowhere near as deep as it looked.

Its darkness suggested a great tank of water, but that darkness was due to the black rock underneath not depth.

How much water did they have? And more to the point, how much time?

He didn't know.

But he knew who did know.

The Sioux.

He doubted the water would last this many people very long.

A few days. Perhaps even several. Call it a week.

But beyond that?

He didn't think so. Not unless God smiled on them, opened the sky, and poured down the first rain in weeks.

"That's all there is?" Sergeant Gentry asked, eyeing the branch.

"That's all."

"Looks deeper."

"It does. Unfortunately, we can't drink looks."

The sergeant nodded grimly.

"Gather around, everyone," Heck called.

The Duncans were standing guard together at the mouth of the passage. Cody was up above on his bench.

Everyone else came over to hear what Heck had to say.

Everyone except Pipher, that is. He'd been sitting on the ground with his back to a boulder, resting in the manner of soldiers everywhere. Now, rather than standing and coming over, he lifted the brim of his hat and stared at Heck with reptilian malice.

"The water level's already dropping," Heck said. He crouched and pointed to where the water line had fallen. "At first glance, the pool looks deep, but that's an illusion created by the dark rock underneath. This is how deep the pool really is."

He held up the branch for all to see.

Folks murmured.

"How long will it last?" Becky asked.

Heck spread his hands. "A few days. Longer, maybe, if we're careful. Which we should be."

"A few days will be plenty," Count Karpov said. "By that time, we will have clashed with the savages and driven them off. We'll be on our way again."

"Why do you assume they'll come at us so quick?"

"Because while we're in here, they're out there." The Count pointed out the passage to the blistering, sun-scorched land beyond. "Whatever we are enduring, they are enduring tenfold."

"You think that'll break them?"

"I think it would break anyone. The heat, the sun, the thirst."

"They have your water barrels, remember?"

"Yes, and the Duncans'. But you forget there are more of them than there are of us. Perhaps three times as many. So that requires three times as much water. More than that, considering they're out in the open."

Heck shook his head. "An Indian can find shade almost anywhere. Trust me. They'll get by on less water than us, even if there are three times as many of them."

"Again," the Count said, "you sound as if you admire them. Perhaps your admiration is exaggerating their capabilities. They are just men after all."

"Just men? In the Sioux tribe, young boys learn to go without food, water, and sleep. By the time they reach manhood, they are as different from you as that buzzard up there."

Heck pointed to the sky, where the lone buzzard wheeled overhead.

"You think too highly of these savages," Count Karpov said. "We will see what they're made of when they come screaming at us. We will slaughter them."

"Come screaming at us, huh?" Heck said with a smile. "Did you read that in a magazine somewhere? Chances are, they'll come creeping up here so quiet, we won't even know they're here until they fire their first volley. But I don't expect a large-scale attack until they're confident that we're running low on water. We need to settle in for the long haul. This means more than just rationing water. We gotta consider pooling our resources."

"My resources belong to me," the Count said. "If you're running low, that's not my problem."

"I am not running low," Heck said. "Considering the circumstances, I'm pretty well set up. But I'm not going to hoard my food or powder. I want the rest of you to be strong enough to keep fighting, too. Otherwise, we're all lost."

"Your pessimism is astounding," the Count said.

"Let's take a vote on it," Heck said. "I say we should pool resources, take an inventory, and then figure out how to make it last."

"You can't vote to take away a man's possessions."

"You had no problem voting whether to take away a man's life. If these folks don't have food and water—"

"Or maybe we should just vote for a leader instead," Cody called down from his perch. "All this bickering is giving me a headache."

This got people to nodding.

Becky, Heck noticed, flashed Cody a bright smile when he proposed the vote.

Heck didn't even have time to wonder why before the blond-haired girl said, "I nominate Count Viktor Karpov."

The Count straightened, and a confident smile spread across his face. "Thank you, Becky. I would be honored to lead this group. Honored and qualified. I might be known for my business dealings, but you should also know that I was educated in some of Europe's finest universities and by father, General Karpov, and on the battlefield, where I led men to not only survive but succeed."

I should have known, Heck thought, taking in the Count's tidy little speech. *He set it all up. He must have gotten Becky to smile at Cody and have the boy propose a vote.*

"I nominate Heck," Sergeant Gentry said. "He knows this country and knows these Indians. I trust him."

Heck nodded. "I accept. I might not be university-educated like the Count, but I've been in tight places before, and I've gotten my people through."

"I vote for the Count," the Countess proclaimed. "He is a great leader. He will save us."

"I stand with Heck," Clarence said. "He's selling himself short. The man's been there and back. If anybody can get us out of here, it's him."

"I did not realize that black men were allowed to vote in this country," the Count said coolly.

"They ain't," Pipher said.

"Nonsense," Sergeant Gentry said. "If he fights, he votes. That's all there is to it. The vote stands at two to two, a tie."

"It ain't no tie, Gentry," Pipher growled. "Me and Pete vote for the Count, ain't that right, Pete?"

Pete looked at Heck then looked at the Count, seeming to think things over. Then he blurted, "That's right, Hank. We vote for the Count."

"So the score is four to two," the Count said with a smile. "Again, five will represent the majority."

"How exciting," Becky said. "Cody? Who do you vote for?"

Cody didn't look up from polishing his rifle barrel. "I vote for Heck."

Becky's mouth dropped wide open, and the Count scowled violently, his cool demeanor completely gone. "Fetch the Duncans."

Saying the farmers' name aloud, a smile returned to the Count's face.

No surprise there. After all, Heck thought, the Duncans had sided with the Count during the last vote.

Pete Twill trotted off to fetch them, and a moment later, Bruce and Mabel Duncan appeared with their young son in tow, having left Pete on guard at the front of the passage.

"Ah, there you are, my friends," the Count said warmly. "In the spirit of democracy, we are voting for someone to lead the group. Four individuals have put their faith in me, and I have pledged to keep them safe. Three people have voted for him. Now, you will decide the vote. If either of you is inclined to support me, you will have chosen the leader."

Bruce Duncan glanced at Heck. There was a touch of calculation in that glance but mostly bitterness, and Heck knew Bruce still resented him, blaming him on some level for all that had befallen his family, and further knew the farmer would cast his vote for the Count.

Bruce Duncan nodded and said, "Well, my vote—"

"We vote for Heck Martin," Mrs. Duncan said boldly.

"What?" Bruce said.

"Heck warned us not to come here in the first place," Mabel Duncan said. Ostensibly, she was speaking to her husband, but because she raised her voice, all could hear, and Heck had the distinct sense that she was speaking to everyone at once.

"Then, when we refused to heed that warning," Mabel continued and swept her eyes across those listening to her, "he left the safety of his home, putting his family in jeopardy to come and try to talk us out of our foolish errand."

"Foolish?" Bruce Duncan said, staring at Mabel as if he'd never seen her before.

"Yes, Bruce, foolish," Mabel said. "Can't you see that now? Can't you see we're only alive because of Heck?"

Bruce Duncan blinked at her for a long second, glanced at Heck, and nodded.

"Mabel's right. I vote for Heck."

"That's it, then," Sergeant Gentry announced. "Five votes to four. Heck Martin is our leader."

CHAPTER 23

V iktor stiffened. His face burned as if he'd been slapped. "Fools!" he snapped. "He'll get us all killed!"

He was filled with rage.

Rage and indignation. How dare these people vote against him?

This was the problem with America. These people and their democracy.

Viktor was born to lead. Born and educated. He had class, money, breeding.

"What are his qualifications?" Viktor shouted.

"We voted for him," Sergeant Gentry said. "That's the only qualification he needs."

Viktor spun on his heel and marched away. His ladies followed.

Still fuming, he led them to the pool.

"Darling," Natalia said, clasping his hand. "It's like you said, my dear husband. They are fools."

"Yeah," Becky agreed. "They—"

"Hush," Viktor said, a bit more sharply than he'd intended to.

The girl's eyes widened, and she stepped back with... what? Surprise? Fear?

He didn't know. But something in him felt more powerful for affecting her so significantly. "Quiet, both of you. We must listen. Who knows what he might propose."

Viktor expected to hear the American gloating, but instead, Heck said, "We gotta set up a watch schedule. We don't have many people, so it's gonna stretch us thin."

Everyone nodded. They looked to Viktor like a bunch of sheep.

"So far, we've just been volunteering," Heck said, "but from here on out, we should have a schedule. That way, everybody will pitch in, and nobody will get worn to a nub. I don't sleep much, so I'll stand extra duty. Anybody else volunteer to take extra shifts?"

Cody raised his hand. "I'll stand extra."

"What happened to the boy?" Viktor asked Becky. "I thought you said he was going to vote for me."

"I'm sorry, Count Karpov. I really thought he would. I mean, he didn't say he would, not in so many words, but he was just so agreeable, and I told him how strong and smart you were."

"Your efforts backfired," Natalia said. "When you talked of Viktor's many strengths, you made the boy jealous."

Becky blushed. "Jealous?"

"Hush, both of you," Viktor said and felt another thrill when Becky dropped her eyes submissively.

Heck was still soliciting volunteers.

"Thanks, Clarence. Thanks, Sergeant Gentry. That'll help. If enough of us volunteer for extra shifts, it will leave fewer time slots for the women."

"You're going to ask the women to stand guard?" Sergeant Gentry said, sounding surprised.

"I am," Heck said. "We need them. They can stand watch up on the ledge, where they are less likely to come under fire. I don't like it any more than you do, but we just don't have enough men to cover two posts, twenty-four hours a day, seven days a week until this over. We need their help."

"I volunteer for extra duty," Mabel Duncan said.

"Mabel," Bruce said, staring at his wife like she was a stranger.

What the man needed to do, Viktor thought, was control her.

For as surprised as he'd been when the boy had voted for Heck, it was the woman who had ultimately destroyed everything.

Some sort of change had come over her. She had seemed like a quiet, dutiful wife when Viktor first met her. Now, she was declaring her vote before her husband and volunteering for guard duty without his consent.

Viktor's mind raced.

He'd had no intention of standing guard duty whatsoever, and if he'd been elected, neither her nor his women would have done so.

But now, with a woman volunteering for extra duty, he had to not only stand guard but also volunteer for extra hours.

He couldn't afford to look weak or cowardly, and that's

exactly how he would look if he slept while Mrs. Duncan stood watch, keeping him safe.

"I volunteer for extra duty as well," Viktor called to the others.

"Thank you, Count Karpov," Heck said. "We can use a man with military experience. Anyone else?"

"Put me down for extra," Bruce said, slipping an arm around his wife's waist.

She smiled at him, turning Viktor's stomach. Melodramatic peasants...

"I'll take an extra shift, too," Becky called out, shocking Viktor.

He laid a hand on her arm. "Becky, my dear child, you are very brave, but you will do no such thing. You need your rest. This has been a very trying ordeal, and unfortunately, I believe things will get even worse. Rest, please."

"No," Becky said. "I'll do my part."

Ultimately, everyone but Natalia and the two deserters, Pipher and Twill, volunteered.

"That's great, everyone," Heck said, panning a smile back and forth across them. "That'll make things a lot better. Sergeant Gentry, I'm sure you've put together a duty roster before."

"Yes, sir," Sergeant Gentry said. "I'll snap right to it."

"Thank you," Heck said. "I'd suggest two-hour blocks. Put the women up on the bench. Put me down for four shifts, more if need be. Make sure I'm at the passage at dawn and dusk, all right?"

"Yes, sir," Sergeant Gentry said, and infuriated Viktor by coming to attention and giving Heck a formal salute.

"Thank you. Now, our next order of business is resources. We're in this together, and I think we need to pool our food, shot, and powder, and get serious about rationing it and the water."

He glanced in Viktor's direction before continuing. "But I know that some of you are opposed. So let's hold another vote. Who thinks we should inventory things, make sure everyone has some food and ammo, and try to ride this thing out together?"

There was no need to count.

Everyone except Viktor and Natalia voted to share.

"Why are voting with them?" Natalia whispered angrily.

"I don't know," Becky said. "It just doesn't seem right, not sharing in a situation like this. I mean, we're all in it together, right?"

"All right, folks," Heck said. "That's great. Luckily, I have a good deal of pemmican and powder. As far as shot goes, I have plenty for my weapons. If you need a different caliber…"

"Natalia," Viktor whispered, leading the women farther from the group. "Hurry to our horses. Take some of the jerky and dried fruit before these thieves search our bags. Hide it away. Quickly."

"Where, dear husband?"

"Anywhere. Just get it out of sight before they take it."

Natalia hurried off without another word, dependable as always.

Becky, on the other hand, stared at him with something like disbelief. "But Count Karpov, that's—"

"Not now," he cut her off. "When the food runs out, you'll thank me, young lady."

CHAPTER 24

Hunger woke Hank Pipher.

He came to on the ground, blinked up into the starless dark of the rimrock overhang, and wanted food.

The inventory had turned up very little to eat.

Pipher and Twill had been running low themselves. Gentry was in even worse shape. The Duncans had nothing at all.

Clarence had some pemmican and hardtack, and the Count had a fair supply of jerky, biscuits, and dried fruit.

The kid had more.

Most of the food belonged to Heck Martin, who set Pipher's teeth on edge.

The guy really thought he was something. Sure, he'd surrendered his food to feed the group, but Pipher was certain Heck had done it mostly to pat himself on the back.

The army was full of guys like him, guys who'd throw themselves into a bullet, hoping someone would call them a hero.

Well, not Pipher. He was his own man and no fool besides.

He would take what he could get and keep on looking out for himself.

Heck had given them each a withered piece of dried fruit, a few strips of jerky, and a biscuit hard enough to bust teeth.

That's what they got for a whole day.

How was Pipher, a two-hundred-pound man, supposed to live on that?

He sat up in the darkness, remembering his plans, remembering why he'd laid his bedroll back by the smaller pools.

Suddenly, he was glad his growling stomach had awakened him.

The Count's lockbox was somewhere back here. He had to poke around and find the thing, so he'd know where the gold was when he decided to ride out of here.

Also, he was curious. And once Pipher got curious about something, it nagged at him.

Pete snored on the hard ground beside him.

Pipher just sat there for a while, studying everything and listening for sounds between Pete's snores.

Most people had bedded down just inside the overhang, but some laid farther out in the main area.

From his position in absolute darkness, Pipher could make out the lumps of sleeping people.

No one was moving.

Good.

Whoever was standing guard at the passage wouldn't see him. Same went for whoever was up top.

He grinned, remembering how people had volunteered for extra duty. What a bunch of morons.

Pipher had expected Gentry to give him the worst duty,

something in the middle of the night, but he'd landed the best duty possible, a two-hour shift in the middle of the afternoon.

His grin stretched even wider when he considered why he'd likely been given that duty.

They didn't trust him. Thought he'd fall asleep on the job or run out on them.

He would never fall asleep on watch, of course, because that might get him killed.

But he had been giving serious thought to running out on them. It would be risky, but so was sitting here, starving to death while the water dried up.

The Indians were probably out there, waiting, but he reckoned he might be able to break through at night, especially if he could steal some extra horses.

Six horses would be good.

That way, he and Pete could ride hard, switch out horses, stay ahead of the Injuns, and switch out again.

As long as they made it into the open, the Injuns would never catch them.

But he wouldn't make a break for it yet. No way. Let the Indians wear down a little. Hopefully, there would be some fighting soon. He'd feel a lot better about his plan if they killed a few Injuns first.

Also, he wouldn't go riding out there empty-handed.

He wouldn't leave until he could take the Count's box with him. He wished he could take the women, too, but that probably wasn't possible.

Also, he'd like to kill Heck, Gentry, and Clarence before pulling out. That kid, too, the one who'd put a rifle on him and Pete when the women had shown up.

But first, he had work to do.

While everyone else slept like babies, he needed to find the box.

He considered waking Pete, but what good would that do?

Sure, he could have him sit there like a lookout, but Pete was jumpy. He was more likely to wake people up than warn Pipher of danger.

Besides, what was the point?

They were all asleep. And if someone did wake up, he'd just say he was being a good soldier and inspecting their defenses.

Moving quietly, he rose and walked to the pool and took a long drink.

Heck had gone on and on about preserving their water.

Well, Pipher sure hoped all those bootlickers were good boys and girls and followed orders because that would mean more water for him.

They were already starving him to death. He wouldn't let them dry him out, too. He had to stay in fighting shape.

After slaking his thirst and drinking a little more for good measure, he walked around the pool and started smoothing his hands over the wall, looking for anything irregular.

At first, he'd considered striking a match because he couldn't see anything. But he hated to make the light, and besides, once he got down to business, he soon realized that darkness was good for this task.

With no light available, he couldn't overlook anything. The darkness forced him to pat every inch of wall from the base to as high as he could reach, along with the stones along the bottom.

It took a while, but he didn't mind. He could be thorough when he cared about something, and he cared about that box.

What he discovered, however, was not the box but a cache of food hidden away.

He thought he recognized it by touch, but then he gave a sniff and finally took a nibble and knew he'd been right.

Jerky and dried apples.

This was the Count's stash. He must've rushed in here and tucked it away before they'd had everyone turn out their goods.

Crafty fella, that Count.

But not crafty enough. Because Pipher had found his stash, and it was significant, probably equal to or greater than the portion the Count had surrendered to the common good.

Pipher could've filled the cave with laughter. Instead, he filled his mouth with jerky and apples, chewing as he shoveled the rest of the stuff into his pockets.

There was a scratching sound behind him, and light enveloped him.

Pipher spun, dropped a handful of jerky, and grabbed the hilt of his knife.

"Don't bother," the Count said. "If you pull the knife, I will blow out your brains."

With most men, Pipher might have called their bluff. He was fast, and most men didn't stand up under pressure.

But there was something in the Count's eyes that stopped him. That and the revolver in the Count's hand.

It was pointed straight at Pipher, and the man stood back far enough that there could be no chance of rushing him before he got off a shot.

Pipher let go of the knife and spread his hands but didn't cower there like some frightened rabbit.

"What do you want?" he asked.

"Put down that food, thief."

"No." Pipher punctuated his refusal by popping an apple slice into his mouth. It tasted great, seasoned as it was by the rage of the Count, who lifted his pistol, aiming it at Pipher's face.

"Go ahead," Pipher said. "Pull the trigger, Count. But what good will it do you? You'll be down a defender. And how will you explain to everyone why you killed me?"

"That isn't your food."

"It isn't yours, either."

"It most certainly is mine."

"Not anymore. Heck Martin confiscated the food, remember? He's bent on slowly starving us, and everybody thinks he's great for it. You make a fuss, I'm gonna holler and wake everyone and laugh while you try to explain why you hid this food."

"You have no right to—"

"Save it, Count. I found it. It's mine."

"No, you can't—"

"What are you gonna do about it?" Pipher said, stuffing the rest of the food into his pocket. "You can't tell anyone because everybody knows who brought this jerky and fruit. In fact, you'd better hope nobody sees me eating this, or they're gonna know you were holding back."

Chuckling to himself, Pipher turned his back on the stammering Count and headed back to his bedroll.

He hadn't found the box yet, but there would be plenty of

time for that. In the meanwhile, he had enough food to last for days, and that meant he could get a good night's sleep. Especially since the idiots had only given him afternoon duty.

This whole situation wasn't turning out to be so bad. Not so bad at all.

CHAPTER 25

"Mr. Martin?" a woman's voice called softly, and Heck was instantly awake.

Mabel Duncan stood over him, her face illuminated by starshine. Overhead, twinkling lights crammed the cold night sky. Under different circumstances, it would have been downright pretty.

"It's time for your watch, sir. It's one in the morning."

"Thank you, Mrs. Duncan. Anything moving out there?"

She frowned and shrugged. "I don't think so. I was staring so hard I was making myself crazy. Sometimes, I thought I saw something moving, but then... nothing."

Heck nodded. "I'd best go relieve Twill. Is someone up top?"

"Yes, sir. I did like you said, woke up Cody, made sure he was on watch, then came down to wake you."

"Good work, Mrs. Duncan, but why are you calling me sir all of a sudden? I'd prefer Heck if it's all the same to you."

"Okay, Heck. It's just I've come to realize I wasn't paying you due respect."

"Huh? You've always been polite to me."

"Polite, yes, but we should have listened to you back in Hope City. And then, all along the way, you were trying to save us."

"That's true," Heck said, "but I was just doing what's right. That doesn't warrant a sir."

"You left your own family to save mine," Mabel said. "If that doesn't warrant a sir, what does? Thank you for that, Heck. Thank you from the bottom of my heart. We should have listened to you sooner, but I can't change that now, so please just know how much I appreciate what you've done—what you're still doing—and know that I will be following your every suggestion from here on out."

"You're welcome, Mrs. Duncan. I'll be happy when this is all over and we're safely returned to civilization. Now, if you're set on following my recommendations, I suggest you go get some sleep."

"Yes, Heck," Mabel said and headed for her sleeping family.

Heck checked his rifle quickly, found everything still in order, and was crossing the enclosure to relieve Pete Twill when Cody's rifle boomed overhead.

A second later, a scream rang out at the end of the passage, followed by the boom of a rifle and another scream.

Heck rushed forward.

As Heck entered the passage, a bloody Pete Twill came running the other way, hunched over and hollering, clutching an arrow poking out of his gut.

"Everyone up!" Heck shouted. "We're under attack!"

Heck hurried to the front of the passage, expecting a Sioux

raiding party, but the passage was empty, and beyond its confines, he could see only darkened scrubland.

Inching forward, rifle at the ready, he reached the end of the passage. He risked a quick glance outside and immediately jerked back as a gunshot split the night. The bullet whined off the stone next to his head.

Another gunshot rang out from overhead, and out in the scrub, a voice cried sharply.

Others arrived, ready to fight alongside Heck.

But the skirmish was already over. There were no more gunshots, no more arrows.

All that was left was Pete Twill's moaning and the panicked murmurs of the others.

CHAPTER 26

Becky was sitting beyond the pools with her back to the wall, right where Count Karpov had told her to sit, when she saw Cody Woodson crouch beside the main pool to fill his canteen.

For a second, she just admired him. He was a good-looking young man, and he moved with confidence. At least until she spoke to him. Whenever she did, he got awful nervous.

Becky knew she had that effect on some boys but could never understand why. The Count and Countess said she was beautiful, but she had never thought of herself that way.

She was just Becky Bonneville, a farm girl from Pennsylvania.

Yes, that's who she was, what she was, not a traveling companion, not some fancy woman destined to marry into wealth.

She didn't even want those things anymore.

She just wanted to go home. She just wanted her old life back.

At first, it had been exciting, saying goodbye to everyone and setting out for the West with a pearl necklace around her throat.

She'd gotten swept up into dreams of a bright future among fancy people in California.

Now, she just wanted to survive, go home, and get back to picking beans and milking cows.

It had all been so exciting, leaving home, and so confusing —confusing enough that for a while, she'd started thinking of her old life, the life of her parents and siblings, as plain and boring and dirty... things she'd never thought when she was living it.

She'd always been happy enough until Count Karpov and his wife came along, called her beautiful, gave her a pearl necklace, and promised her a new and wonderful life in a far-off land.

She'd been a fool. It filled her with shame, realizing how she had betrayed her own life.

Now, watching Cody fill his canteen, she wanted very badly to talk to him. He reminded her of home and her father.

Not that he looked like her father.

Cody was just a boy, after all.

But he was the same sort of person, only younger. A strong, sensible, young man who knew his way around.

She called to him.

Cody looked up with confusion. "Oh, hi, Becky. What are you doing all the way back there?"

"Nothing," she said, realizing how ridiculous she must look, sitting all alone over here in the dark. "Want to come over and visit?"

"Sure," Cody said, and then he was coming toward her.

She watched him as he walked around the main pool. He really was handsome. Not in an exotic, refined way, like the Count.

No, Cody looked like a boy she might have met back home. And something else, she realized, as he came around one of the smaller pools, smiling nervously.

He looked nice.

Which was something she would never think about the Count again.

Yes, the Count had been nice to her when they first met, giving her the necklace and offering her what had seemed like the chance of a lifetime, and he'd been polite enough as they'd traveled together, but she'd seen a different side of him since coming here to this place.

And he certainly hadn't been nice to the others. He'd argued with Mr. Martin a few times, once because he didn't want to share his food.

Which might have been understandable in some fancy castle or something. But here? These people needed food to survive.

And then, after the people had elected Mr. Martin as their leader, the Count had gone against him and hidden away half their food.

Becky had been mortified. Even though she'd had nothing to do with it, she felt horribly guilty.

Then, in the middle of the night, the loathsome Mr. Pipher had sniffed out the cache and stolen the food.

Which is why she was sitting here now. The Count and

Countess were off doing guard duty, so she was supposed to sit against the rocks hiding the Count's precious gems.

He'd shown them to her once along the trail. She knew practically nothing of such things, but she'd heard of some of the names he'd mentioned—diamonds, emeralds, rubies—and besides, a girl didn't need to know anything about gemstones to be dazzled.

And dazzled she had been. By the jewels and by the Count and Countess.

Now, not so much. She no longer knew exactly how she felt about the Count and Countess. She only knew that things weren't so simple as she had foolishly first imagined, and the count wasn't quite so strong or honorable as she had assumed.

As to the gems, she'd trade the whole box if she could just snap her fingers and be back on the farm.

That, of course, was impossible, but at least she could talk to someone who reminded her of home, someone she thought she might understand.

"Trying to stay cool back here?" Cody asked with a smile.

"Something like that," Becky said. "Want to sit down?"

"You sure you don't mind?"

"I asked you, didn't I, silly?"

"All right." He sat down across from her a few feet away. "How are you holding up?"

"I'm okay, thanks. Missing home a little."

"Just a little?"

"Okay, a lot. I sure wish I was home."

"Where you from?"

"Wysox, Pennsylvania. Ever heard of it?"

"No, ma'am."

"It's real nice. We're not far from Towanda?"

He just looked at her, and she realized he had never heard of Towanda, either.

Imagine that, having never heard of Towanda?

Even as these thoughts flashed through her mind, they were chased by another realization: until recently, her world had been very small, defined by a handful of miles among the Endless Mountains of northern Pennsylvania.

Yes, very small indeed—and heartbreakingly lovely.

"Are you okay?" Cody asked.

"Yes, just thinking of home. Towanda is a big town on the Susquehanna River. There used to be a lot of Indian trouble a long time ago—Queen Esther and the Iroquois?"

Again, he just looked at her.

"But it's real nice now," she said. "Towanda is the county seat. It's up and coming. Fifteen hundred people live there. Can you believe it? Fifteen hundred. Why, not long ago, Towanda barely had a thousand." She laughed. "And now I'm babbling like an idiot."

"No, you ain't. I asked. I like hearing about it."

"Where are you from, Cody?"

"Tennessee, originally. But my family was never one for sinking roots, I guess. We moved here and there, ended up in Texas. I liked it down there, but Ma got killed by Comanches, and Pa, he got killed by a bull."

"Oh, Cody, I'm so sorry."

He shrugged. "Thanks. I miss them."

"Do you miss home, too?"

"Texas? Nah. It wasn't really home after Ma died. And then, when Pa died, well, I didn't see no reason to hang around. I'm the youngest of six. They all started their lives already. My brother got me a job at the mercantile where he worked, but I couldn't work in no store, be cooped up, smell the same smells day after day. No thank you, ma'am."

"Well, I'll bet you wish you were back there now, anyway, even if you had to work in a store."

Cody tilted his head and gave her a funny look. "Why?"

"Well, because of this mess we're in, silly."

"Oh, yeah. Well, don't you worry, Becky. We'll get out of this. I promise."

"You promise, huh?"

"Yes, ma'am. I promise to see you through."

"Well thank you, sir."

They were quiet for a time, and Becky smiled, feeling something between them.

Something good, like friendship, only warmer.

She liked Cody. He was a comfort. And nice, too, but not just nice. Strong as well.

"I heard you were on duty when the Indians attacked last night."

He nodded. "One of them came over the wall, quiet as a cat. It was weird. Took me a second to believe my eyes. Well, not a full second, but you know what I mean. There was no sound, not even a scrape. One second, everything was normal. The next, he's pulling himself on top of the boulder across from me."

"That must have been terrifying!"

"No, ma'am. Not really. It was a surprise. But fear didn't play into it. There wasn't any time to be scared. I just lifted my rifle and pulled the trigger."

"Did you hit him?"

Cody nodded. "In the chest, I think. That's what I was aiming for, anyway, and he tumbled back over the side."

"Was he killed, then?"

"I reckon so. If getting shot in the chest didn't kill him, the fall should have."

"But there wasn't a body out there this morning."

"No, ma'am. The Sioux honor their dead. A lot of Indians are that way. They try not to leave the dead behind."

"Why?"

He spread his hands. "That's their business, not mine. But tribes have their own rituals, just like we do. I hear the Sioux wrap them up and build scaffolds and put them up there a while."

She was happy that he was growing more comfortable around her because she liked listening to him talk.

"I think I hit another one out in the scrub, too. He hollered like I did, anyway."

Becky smiled.

Cody really was strong. She knew he meant his promise to keep her safe.

She believed it, too.

And that was worth more than any pearl necklace.

CHAPTER 27

"What are doing, Mr. Martin?" a tiny voice asked.

Crouched beside the main pool, Heck swiveled around and found himself face-to-face with young Simon Duncan.

"Checking the water level, Simon."

"Is it okay?"

Heck smiled. "It's okay."

Which was the truth. For today. And maybe a few more days.

But the water was dropping faster than he would have expected. There was no reason to share that, however, with a child. The kid had enough to worry about as it was.

"Do you think the Indians will attack again today?"

"Maybe," Heck said. "It's hard to tell with Indians. The men we face are part of the Sioux tribe, and they are very smart."

The boy looked more worried than ever.

"Good thing we're smart, too," Heck said with a smile.

"Don't worry, son. We're gonna get through this. We have water, we have a strong position, and everybody's working together."

"What can I do?" Simon asked, and once again, Heck was reminded of his oldest son, Tor, who always followed him around, wanting to help.

"Right now, you just listen to your parents, do what they say, and pray to God for help."

"Yes sir, I'll do that."

"Good man. Tell you what, Simon. We get out of here and go back to Hope City, how would you like some more candy?"

The boy's face lit up, all fear temporarily wiped away by the thought of sweets. "I'd love it, sir!"

"All right, then," Heck laughed, patting Simon on the back. "You be a good boy, listen to your parents, and say your prayers, and I'll fetch you some candy as soon as we get home."

The boy thanked him and ran off excitedly, probably to tell his mother, who was drowsing on the other side of the pool. Bruce Duncan was on guard duty at the front of the passage.

Heck took one more look at the water line. It was definitely lower than he would have expected.

Of course, those expectations were wild conjecture at best. There were a lot of people here and horses, too, and the heat of the day was great, stealing yet more.

But he remembered the Count telling his women to drink as much as possible and had no doubt that Pipher would drink more than his allotment for the sheer fun of being insubordinate.

Wherever the water was going, it was going, and that changed things.

Instead of weeks, they had days.

And what did that mean? What could they do?

They couldn't run for it. The Sioux would expect that.

Besides, they didn't have enough horses. Not for all of them.

Red was still in good shape, but most of these horses were worn thin. Very thin.

From the shade under the rimrock, Pete Twill moaned. It was a terrible sound. Twill was unconscious, and the mournful, agonized noise that came out of him was somehow even more horrible for its involuntary nature.

Becky got up from where she and the Count had been sitting against the far wall and came over and knelt beside Twill.

Heck ambled over.

Becky murmured to Twill, whose only response was more moaning, and held a hand to his forehead.

She frowned then looked up at Heck. "He's feverish."

"Makes sense. He's hurt bad."

"Yes, sir. I hate to hear him cry out like that. Should we wake him?"

"No. He needs every bit of rest he can get."

Becky lowered her voice to a whisper. "Will he live?"

"Hard to tell," Heck said. "This is a bad place to get shot. Wish we were back in Hope City. We have a doctor and medicine, and my wife's a good nurse. I don't know if they could save him, but it sure would up his chances."

"What's she like?" Becky asked.

"Who?"

"Your wife."

"Hope? Why, she's the greatest woman I've ever known.

She's smart and skilled and hardworking, a great mother and a help to the community. She loves Jesus, puts her family before herself, and never complains. And brave? You never met anybody braver."

Becky smiled. "She sounds like quite a woman."

"Oh, she is that. She is quite a woman."

"A change came over you when you spoke of her. I never saw you look like that, like you were full of light."

Heck chuckled. "Is that right? Well, it makes sense, I guess, because that's how Hope makes me feel: full of light. Don't get me started on my kids, or I might shine bright enough to blind you."

Becky laughed. "How many children do you have, Mr. Martin?"

"Three out and about with another on the way. Two boys, a girl, and the other we'll soon meet."

"You're shining even brighter. You must love them very much."

"You got no idea. There is nothing I wouldn't do for those children."

"My daddy's that way. I got a whole slew of brothers and sisters. There's thirteen of us. Just the kids, I mean. Mama and Daddy make fifteen. So we never had much, but we get by."

"Folks do."

"Yes, sir. Daddy works from sunup to sundown every day. Mama, too. Most of us kids, too, except Todd. He's soft in the head. Born that way. But mostly, we all work hard."

"You miss home," he said.

"Yes, Mr. Martin, I do."

"It shows. What you said—about me changing when I talked

about Hope and the kids—well, a change came over you when you started talking about your family, too."

"I miss them terribly. I wish I was home now."

He wanted to ask why she'd left in the first place but reckoned it was none of his business. If she wanted to volunteer that story, she would.

Instead, Becky asked, "Mr. Martin, do you think I'll ever see home again?"

"Is that what you want?"

"More than anything."

"Then yes, I think you'll see home again."

"Do you think maybe someday I might…" she paused, blushing, then carried on, "… meet a man and get married—I mean a man who loves me the way you love your wife?"

"Becky, I believe you can do whatever you like." He glanced past her into the gloom beneath the rimrock, where the Count sat staring at him with angry eyes. "But you gotta be real careful who you hitch your wagon to. If it's a good man you want, don't settle for less. And don't let other things fool you."

"Things like money?"

"Yes, ma'am."

"Or fancy stuff?"

"Ma'am?"

"Like titles and stories about fancy parties?"

"Right. A man doesn't need money to be good, though most good men, given time, build a stake through hard work and honest dealings and the favor of the Almighty."

"How will I know him?"

"You'll know him. And you won't need me or anybody else to tell you, so long as you are honest with yourself. A good man won't need to tell you stories. You'll know he's good by the way he treats you and the way he walks through life, especially when the hard times come. That, more than anything else. When hard times come, good men stand firm and face the trouble head on. Other men stand behind them… or run."

"I thank you for your time, Mr. Martin, and for talking to me. It's given me hope."

She smiled up at him, but Twill set to moaning again, reminding them of the hard road ahead.

Overhead, the buzzard circled.

CHAPTER 28

The day wore tortuously on. The sun burned like a huge furnace in the brassy sky, baking the dry land, cracking it, crumbling the world to dust, and testing the nerves of those who clung to shadows within Petit Wells.

There were no additional attacks throughout the morning.

The Countess asked if that meant the Indians had retreated, scared off, perhaps, by the previous night's skirmish.

"No," Viktor said. "If anything, last night's skirmish will embolden the savages."

"But why? Two were hit, possibly killed."

"Because they are savages," Viktor snapped.

He was tired of sitting there on the ground, guarding the box. He wanted to be away from here, in California, riding across a beautiful estate, enjoying a new world full of promise.

But instead, he was stuck here, guarding that future from a low-born thief, a man with no principles, no decency whatsoever.

As if summoned by these thoughts, Hank Pipher appeared on the other side of the big pool, grinned at Viktor, then gave a little salute.

Next, the hulking miscreant reached inside his filthy uniform and, glancing quickly to either side, lifted an apple slice to his grinning mouth and tossed it in whole.

That's my apple, Viktor thought bitterly. *And my jerky.*

Pipher stood there, chewing and grinning, rubbing it in Viktor's face.

"He'll try to take the gems," Viktor whispered to his wife. "I'm sure of it."

"What will you do?"

"I'm not certain."

"Will you force him into a duel?"

"Perhaps. It would be most enjoyable. But the others would surely frown on such a duel, given the fact that we are short on defenders, especially with Twill moaning on the ground over there."

"I wish he would hurry up and die," the Countess said.

"As do I, darling. Even if he recovers, it won't be in time to help us, so his survival has no point. Meanwhile, he drinks our water and grates our nerves with his ceaseless whimpering."

"It's making me terribly anxious," the Countess complained. "Someone should put him out of his misery. But darling, what are we going to do?"

"Wait and hope for an attack, an all-out assault that will maximize our defensive position. Even with Twill down, I believe we can beat them back."

"Why don't they attack?"

"I must assume that Heck Martin was right about that much,

at least. These savages must be smarter than I thought. More cunning, anyway. They seem to be waiting us out."

"Waiting for what? Nightfall?"

"How should I know the mind of a savage? Perhaps nightfall, or perhaps they are simply better set for water than we are, as Heck Martin suggested."

"And if that's the case, all they need to do is wait?"

"Correct. They will wait for thirst to weaken us, then attack."

"Why then, even? Why risk an attack, when they could simply wait longer and let us die of thirst?"

"Because they want us alive, my dear. Particularly you and Becky and the Duncan woman."

Natalia shuddered with revulsion and produced the derringer from the folds of her dress, which now, thanks to the heat and dust, looked like a heap of wilting flowers. "I will not let it come to that. But speaking of Becky, where is she? Shouldn't she be off duty by now?"

"Yes," he said, and something in him shifted like a crocodile in a swamp smelling blood. "In fact, I saw the boy go up the rope ladder ten minutes ago, maybe later. He was to relieve her."

He stood.

"Are you going to go fetch her, dear husband?"

"I am."

"Good. I don't like that boy. I've seen Becky talking to him a few times. Talking and smiling."

"I've noticed that, too. It irks me. It lessens her, don't you think? Makes her seem like a commoner."

"She is a commoner, darling."

"Yes, but she doesn't have to act like one. I'm going up there."

Leaving the shade, Viktor was struck by the sunlight, which seemed even brighter and hotter today. He shielded his eyes and squinted for a moment, temporarily blinded, then opened them slowly beneath the visor of his uplifted hand, letting them adapt.

Meanwhile, the sun beat down, burning his skin, making him sweat, then wicking away the perspiration, as if it were trying to wither and weaken and destroy him.

Up the rope ladder he went, irritation building in him as he reached the bench and could hear the two young people talking from the guard position up above.

"My brother Claude," Becky said, "he can call a turkey with his voice. He's little so he still has a high-pitched voice. I swear, he sounds just like a hen turkey, and those big toms come a running. Pa calls Claude his secret weapon."

The two of them laughed like a pair of idiots.

Viktor climbed the rest of the way up and saw them sitting there together—much too close for his liking.

"Becky," he said, allowing impatience to fill his voice as he straightened to his full height. "The Countess and I supposed you had finished your watch."

Becky's laughter died, but she kept smiling. "Oh, I did, Count Karpov. I was just talking with Cody is all."

Viktor frowned down at her.

Becky's dress was in a sorry state. As were her blond curls. Beneath the pearls, her throat was mottled with dust.

The illusion was fading. Before him now was the real Becky: a peasant girl he'd plucked from a filthy brood of peasant children, a cur of a young woman who just happened to possess a pretty face and a shapely figure.

She was beneath him.

It enraged Viktor and excited him, made him angry at himself and Becky and his father, without whose inflexibility and harsh criticism none of this would even be happening. Because if Viktor hadn't quarreled with the General, he'd still be in Russia or perhaps touring Europe, living the good life and yes, occasionally amusing himself with a peasant girl—but not saddling himself with one so common and ungrateful.

But he had set his course, and he would not lose her now.

"Come along, Becky," he said, trying and failing to keep the anger out of his voice. "The Countess and I are preparing to eat."

"I'd rather stay up here if you don't mind, Count Karpov. Cody's been helping me to stop thinking about—"

"As it just so happens, I do mind," Viktor said. "In case you have forgotten, we are traveling companions, and traveling companions dine together."

Becky gave him a look then that he would never have expected from her, a look that blended annoyance and something else, something approaching disdain.

"Eat what?" she asked. "Jerky and hardtack? It's not like we're sitting down to a seven-course dinner."

"You're coming with me," he said, ending the matter, and started to reach for her, when the boy, who'd been sitting there with no expression on his face, finally spoke.

"Mister, it sounds to me like she don't want to go."

Suddenly, all Viktor's frustrations ignited, filling him with hot fire and the need to destroy this stupid young man. "How dare you question me, boy?"

The kid didn't even blink. If he was afraid, he wasn't showing it. He stood to his full height, which was almost equal to that of Viktor, and thanks to his position on the boulder, he looked down at Viktor.

"Shucks, buddy, I didn't think twice about it. Seems to me you're trying to push this girl. If she doesn't want to go, you'd best clear out."

Suddenly, Viktor was wild with rage, and the things that had been holding him back no longer mattered. Not Becky's opinion of him, the reaction of this ridiculous group, or even the number of defenders to fight against the savages. All that mattered to him now was making this lowly young worm pay for his impudence.

Viktor lifted his chin and pointed at the stupid boy. "You, sir, have offended me. My honor demands that you face me in a duel… to the death."

Shockingly, the boy grinned at him. "What, count out ten paces and have at it? Sounds like sissy stuff to me. You want to fight, go for it, buddy. But before you get that big Colt out of its holster, I'm gonna kick you square in the chest, and you will go over backward. It's a pretty good fall down to the bench, and I reckon about the time you hit it, I'll blow a hole through the middle of you."

Viktor turned to see that he was, indeed, standing at the very edge of the boulder. Realizing the boy's vicious threat was viable, Viktor lifted his chin higher still, disguising the sudden rush of fear that frosted his spine.

What if he'd actually struck the boy, as he'd considered doing?

Well, then he'd be dead, killed by a nobody in a pile of rocks in the middle of nowhere. What an inglorious way to die.

"You, sir, have no honor," Viktor said, his voice trembling with impotent rage.

The kid shrugged. "I get by."

Viktor turned to Becky and held out his hand. "Come along, Becky, right now, unless you'd like to lose your position as our traveling companion."

For as shocking as this whole interaction had been, what happened next shocked Viktor more than anything.

Becky shook her head. "Here," she said, standing and untying the pearl necklace from around her throat then handing it to him. "I quit. You aren't who I thought you were. And I'm not who you want me to be. I'm not some fancy lady. Never was, never will be. I'm just plain old Becky, a farm girl from Pennsylvania, and that's all I ever want to be."

CHAPTER 29

The day grew hotter and hotter.

Even Heck, who was powerfully conditioned to extreme temperatures, felt it.

He'd finished his watch at the front of the passage. Nothing was moving out there, and he had seen no dust clouds in the distance that might herald the arrival of help from afar.

Now, he was taking a break in the shade under the rimrock.

His stomach growled.

He leaned back on an elbow, resting, and took a small bite of jerky and a quick drink from his canteen, which remained mostly full.

Pipher was on watch down below. Mabel Duncan was up top.

Mabel's family was a short distance away. Bruce Duncan was using pebbles to play a game of marbles with Simon.

It was good to hear the boy's laughter and good to see his father looking happy and alert.

Immediately after the Duncans' wagon had burned, Bruce seemed to slip into a semi-conscious state. For a while there, all he would do was stand and stare out at the charred remains of his life.

Heck figured Bruce was wrestling with a lot then, not just the loss of his possessions but also the knowledge that this was all his fault. His family was in danger because he had made bad moves. Very bad moves.

Heck wasn't sure that night if Bruce would recover.

But the man was doing better today. Much better, in fact, and Heck thanked God for that.

They needed Bruce, just as they needed everyone, but more than that, his family needed him.

Clarence napped a short distance away, getting rest while he could. The man was a survivor, that was for sure.

Pete Twill went back and forth between sleeping fitfully and screaming about the pain.

Becky lingered near the wounded man, tending to him as best she could and chatting with Cody.

Despite the heat and constant menace, the pair talked non-stop and seemed remarkably happy.

Which was quite a contrast to the Count and Countess, who still sat at the back of the cave, looking absolutely miserable.

Had they had some kind of falling out with Becky?

Heck hoped so for the girl's sake.

Sergeant Gentry sat ten feet away to Heck's left, staring blankly out into the enclosure. He looked grizzled and tired.

As Heck was registering these things, the old soldier stood and shuffled out of the shade and across the enclosure to relieve Pipher at the front of the passage.

At the same time, without a word from anyone, Clarence, who'd been lying there with the hat down over his eyes, sat up, straightened his hat, nodded to Heck, and set off for the rope ladder to relieve Mabel Duncan.

Both men seemed smaller, shabbier, and wearier once they stepped into the blazing sunlight.

Were the Sioux uncomfortable, too?

They had to be.

But how uncomfortable?

Uncomfortable enough to pull out of here?

Not likely. Not with women and horses at stake.

He wondered what was happening back in Hope City and wished he knew. If help was on its way, that would change everything.

In that case, it would just be a waiting game.

But without that knowledge, they would get weaker and more desperate by the day.

They would still be sitting there, waiting for nothing, when the water ran out. And when they ran out of water, they would also run out of time.

He revisited the notion of making a break for it, getting everyone mounted up, some of them doubled, and charging into the darkness.

The decisive idea appealed to him. The thought of plunging into darkness and fighting it out with a tangible opponent sure would beat sitting here, sweating, and getting weaker and thirstier every day.

But it was a desperate fantasy, a simple answer when the real truth was complex and uncertain and bleaker by the moment.

They didn't have enough horses, and even if they did, they would have to break through the Indians' line. Then, the Sioux would pursue them all the way to the next well, a distance of nearly thirty miles.

So they had to wait.

Wait for what, though?

For the Sioux to get impatient?

Not likely.

For someone to come to their rescue?

Again, not likely.

For what, then?

For something to change. That was it. For something to change enough that one course of action made the most sense.

But Heck knew that waiting for change was not a plan. Victory seldom went to the passive.

He had to think, had to come up with a new idea, had to—

Shouting erupted at the front of the passage.

Heck was up in an instant and sprinting across the enclosure toward the passage, out of which Pipher's voice bellowed, "You just try it, old man, and I'll knock your teeth out."

As Heck reached them, Sergeant Gentry lashed out with the butt of his rifle.

Pipher, moving with the speed of a much smaller man, ducked the blow and drove a fist into Gentry's stomach. He followed this with a looping hook that smashed into the sergeant's jaw.

Gentry stumbled into the boulder, badly hurt, and gunshots erupted outside the passage.

CHAPTER 30

R ounds smashed into the boulders and whined, ricocheting in all directions.

Pipher shouted, clapped a hand to his face, and ran past Heck, abandoning his post and his rifle.

Sergeant Gentry hollered and fell to the ground, clutching his leg.

Heck rushed forward and crouched beside Gentry, staring out the mouth of the passage, ready for an attack. "You okay, Gentry?"

"All right," Gentry growled, dragging himself back several feet and getting his own rifle into position. "Hit my knee. Don't know if I can walk, but I can darn well fight."

A gunshot sounded from overhead, Clarence firing his rifle.

Was Clarence firing out into the desert, or were they coming over the walls?

Voices shouted within the enclosure and Heck heard footsteps as defenders rushed forward.

But then there was a curious whooshing sound like birds cutting the wind, rushing toward them.

"Arrows!" Heck shouted.

He heard arrows clatter off boulders and heard screams from people who'd been struck.

The Sioux had been waiting for someone to get careless.

The fight between Gentry and Pipher had given them the opportunity to open fire on the passage. Which, in turn, had brought the others running.

Just as the Sioux had known it would.

Their archers had probably been lying out there for hours. When the gunshots came, they finally rose and lobbed a volley of arrows over the wall and into the running defenders.

"Is this it, you reckon?" Gentry asked. "They coming for us?"

"I don't know, but I doubt it."

There was another whoosh and more arrows, but no new cries from the enclosure.

A moment later, more arrows. Then, a fourth volley.

From up on the bench, Clarence's rifle boomed. "I hit one," he reported.

Then, a break in the action. No more shooting, no more arrows.

Heck wiped stinging sweat from his eyes and waited in the blistering sun, ready for an attack.

But the moment stretched on and on, and after several minutes, it seemed there would be no charge.

Which made sense, of course.

The Sioux had executed a clever, successful attack. They knew they had shed blood and, just as importantly, rattled the defenders.

The whole Sioux culture was built around self-control. From early childhood, Sioux boys were expected to master themselves. Self-control began with silence and developed through deprivation and silent suffering.

Comfort was scorned; pain was welcomed; fear was mocked. And through all those hard, silent years, the boys heard tales of great warriors, men who endured, men who thought on their feet, man who fought shrewdly and well and won.

Meanwhile, they were taught the ways of war from birth. Young boys competed against one another in wrestling and fought with mock knives and challenged each other in a wide array of contests: running, riding, jumping, swimming, and, of course, archery.

Sioux boys mastered their bows at a very early age and constantly tried to outshoot one another, trying to fire the fastest, skewer a crow on the wing, or knock a bug from a leaf.

So yes, they were formidable warriors, but what made them most dangerous now was not their physical prowess or skill with weaponry; it was their self-mastery.

Having scored a victorious blow, they would not succumb to excitement and rush forward.

No, this was a war of attrition. The Sioux were not seeking a swift kill, Heck understood.

They were like a pack of wolves taking a bull elk, barking and nipping, loping after him, giving him no rest, chasing him over mile after mile of hard country, working together, wearing him down, never taking unnecessary risks, their panting mouths all but smiling as the elk grew weaker and weaker, losing its will to live; until finally, exhausted, it collapsed and stumbled back to its feet only to be hamstrung, taken down, and torn to pieces, its great size and strength rendered meaningless by patience, endurance, and a simple, foolproof plan.

CHAPTER 31

"No, I insist," Sergeant Gentry said. With Heck's help, he was sitting up on a stone with his bad leg propped atop another, just back from the mouth of the passage, where he could cover everything without exposing himself to the enemy. "You go ahead and talk to folks. They'll be wanting to hear from you. Fact is, I reckon they need to hear from you."

"Well, I can send somebody forward to take your shift."

"No, sir. I'll stand my watch. The bleeding's slowed considerably. Round went in and out."

"Hit bone?"

"Hit and grazed off. Hurts but I'm not in danger of bleeding out. I'll stand watch. Or sit it, anyway."

"All right, Sergeant," Heck said. "I'll leave you to it, then."

Gentry nodded, but as Heck was turning to leave, the old sergeant spoke again. "I'm sorry, Heck."

"What for?"

"For tangling with Pipher. If I hadn't done that…"

Heck nodded. "It was foolish. And yes, they made us pay."

"When I came here to relieve him—"

"I don't even want to hear about it," Heck interrupted. "No matter what Pipher says, you gotta leave it alone until this is over. Understand? We need everybody, even Pipher, if an assault comes."

"Yes, sir. I'll ignore him until this is over. But then—"

"Don't even tell me," Heck said. "That's between the two of you."

He turned and went into the enclosure, where everyone was gathered by the dwindling pools under the rimrock.

And they were dwindling. At the rate they were dropping, they might only have water left for two or three days.

Pete Twill had come to and was shouting about the pain.

Becky crouched at Twill's side, trying and failing to comfort the screaming man.

The others ignored Twill. They had surrounded Pipher, who faced them as belligerently as a wolf at bay.

"I'm telling you," Pipher said, "the old man started it."

"And the Indians finished it," Clarence said.

"Clarence is right," Heck said, reaching the group. "We slipped up, and the Sioux pounced."

"Pounced?" the Count said with disdain. "They fired their weapons from a distance, like cowards. If they had *pounced*, as you put it, this would all be over. They would have come in here and fought like men, and we would have routed them."

"Wouldn't make any sense for them to do that," Bruce Duncan said, holding a bloody rag to his arm. "Heck's right. We gave them an advantage, and they made the most of it."

The Count glared at Bruce Duncan for an instant then seemed to notice the rest of the group and straightened, visibly composing himself.

"You must all pardon my emotion," the Count said. "I concede, Mr. Martin, that these savages are fighting shrewdly. Their manner of fighting is an affront to me. Where I am from, men meet face-to-face and settle their differences honorably. I apologize for speaking so rashly."

"No problem, Count," Heck said. "Look, we're all in a tough spot here. But we gotta stick together."

"With one exception," Count Karpov said. "Him." He pointed at Pipher.

"What about me?" Pipher challenged.

"When I suggested mercy, I truly believed that you would do your best to earn your pardon, Mr. Pipher," the Count said, "but you clearly respect nothing, not even your own life. You have been nothing but a thorn in our side this entire time, and now, you have dealt us a terrific blow, all because you started a fight over a personal grievance."

"I already told you," Pipher snarled. "I didn't start the fight. Gentry did."

"No one believes you," the Count said. "In light of Private Pipher's continued insubordination and damaging actions, I move that we revoke his pardon immediately and bring justice swiftly—before he gets us all killed."

The others murmured in support.

Pipher took a step back. His eyes narrowed, jumping from face to face. Seeing their intention, he yanked the knife from his belt. Having abandoned his rifle at the mouth of the passage, it was the best weapon he had. "Stay away from me. I didn't start the fight!"

Suddenly, the Count's Navy Colt was in his hand, aimed at Pipher's chest. "Put down the knife, Pipher."

Pipher laughed. "He just wants me dead because I know about the gold!"

CHAPTER 32

People whispered among themselves, wondering aloud about the gold Pipher had mentioned.

"Gold?" the Count said and turned to the others with an incredulous expression. "This man is a liar!"

"It's back in the cave against the wall in a lockbox," Pipher said, grinning. "That's why him and the Countess sit there all the time. Look, she's back there right now."

The murmuring grew louder.

"Even if I had gold, that would be no business of yours, Pipher," the Count snapped. "Or anyone else's. What's mine is mine."

"Like this food?" Pipher said, pulling a fistful of jerky and apple slices from his pocket and tossing them into the air.

Heck's stomach growled just seeing the food. Like everyone else, he was very hungry.

"You're a thief, Pipher!" the Count shouted.

"He hid this stuff in the cave, too, after Heck told us to turn in all our food. The Count held back all this food, and—"

"Don't listen to his lies!" the Count said. "You started the fight, and you must die. Now. No one believes you!"

"I believe him," Heck said. "I talked to Gentry. He apologized for stirring things up."

"Ha!" Pipher sheathed his knife and pointed at the Count, laughing. "Nice try!"

"What I'd like to hear more about is this food you squirreled away," Heck said. "We had an agreement."

"We never had an agreement," the Count snapped. He took a step forward, his gun swiveling toward Heck. "I gave these people half my food. Half! The rest I held back to use as I saw fit."

"We would have shared it when the food ran out," the Countess called absurdly from her post along the wall.

"Yes, we would have, but this thief stole it."

"Pick it up, then," Heck said, "and add it to the communal supply."

"How dare you tell me what to do?" the Count said.

He lifted his pistol and aimed straight at Heck's chest. His eyes were wild with anger, but his hand was steady. At this range, he couldn't miss.

"You are not fit to lead this group," the Count declared. "We're coming apart at the seams, and it's all for want of a strong leader. Well, I am that strong leader. You, with all your talk of how wonderful the savages are and how we just need to wait… what has it gotten us? Nothing. Worse than nothing. We are weaker than ever, and the water is racing away. You are hereby relieved of duty."

A second later, Cody and Clarence had their rifles pointed at the Count.

Heck walked straight at the Count, who did not drop his weapon. "If you pull that trigger, you're dead. Understand, Count?"

"And you will be, too."

"Right," Heck said, reaching him. The muzzle was an inch from his chest. "But you might as well just shoot yourself in the head because you'll be just as dead.

"That's what you gotta get into your head. We are in this together. You have some notion that things should be the way you want them to be, but that's not real.

"The Sioux are real. Hunger and thirst are real. Death is real. And it'll come for you just like it'll come for any of us, with no regard to gold or titles or what you want. Now, put down your gun and quit acting like a child."

The Count's face twitched with rage, and now his hand was shaking, not from nerves but from the effort of restraining himself.

The Count very much wanted to shoot Heck. But he didn't want to be killed by Cody and Clarence.

He dropped the weapon and lowered his gaze to the ground.

"The same goes for all of us," Heck said. "We can't let the heat and pressure get to us. We gotta stick together. And that includes you, Pipher. Stop fighting us and start fighting beside us. It's our only chance."

"People leave me alone, I'll leave them alone," Pipher said.

"Give up the rest of the food," Heck said. "We need every bit of food and water if we're gonna make it. We can't be selfish. If one of us dies, we are all more vulnerable."

Everyone was silent for a moment, contemplating his words.

Then, with the perfect timing of a dark omen, Pete Twill cried out for his mother, choked violently, and died on the ground beside them.

CHAPTER 33

"Anyone have a shovel?" Bruce Duncan asked the group. His question made Becky cry all the harder. "Oh, the poor man. The poor, poor man, dying here, dying like this!"

Bruce didn't know why the girl was crying over a ne'er-do-well like Pete Twill, who, from all accounts, had been ready to abuse her until Cody stopped him; but he supposed she was just fragile and had a kindly nature and might even be feeling a touch sorry for herself.

It was a shocking thing, this death, a reminder of how precarious their survival was here.

Three men had now been injured while watching the passage. Now, one of them had died. It was a dangerous duty.

But then again, he thought, feeling the burn where the arrow had scored his arm, *there is no safe place here.*

A few people shook their heads in response to his question, which Cody repeated, "Anybody got a shovel?"

No one did.

Bruce stomped his foot on the ground. "No way to dig here. Ground's hard as a rock. What will we do with him?"

"We should bury him back in the shade," Becky said, sniffing. "It's the least we can do for the poor man."

"No, ma'am," Clarence said in a soft voice. "That won't do, not so close to the water."

Becky started sobbing all over again.

"Should we lay him over by the passage, off to one side?" Bruce asked. "We could cover him over with rocks."

"No way," Cody said. "Can you imagine the stink?"

"Cody's right," Heck said. "I hate to say it, but we can't bury him, and we can't build him a cairn. We have to put him over the side."

Becky gasped. "You can't be serious."

"I'm sorry, Becky," Heck said. "I truly am. I don't mean to dishonor the dead. But we've got to think about the living."

"But does that mean," Becky said, looking at him with huge eyes. "That if…" She trailed off and set to sobbing again.

Cody went to her side and put a hand on her shoulder, and she latched onto it like a drowning woman grabbing hold of a lifeline.

Bruce understood her unfinished question. She was concerned that if she died, they would toss her over the side like so much trash to rot in the sun.

The answer, of course, was yes… yes, they would.

If any of them died, it was all they could expect.

Not long ago, this idea would have troubled Bruce. He'd always expected to die at home, surrounded by his loved ones, and to be planted in the ground not far from his house and visited from time to time, the way he frequently sneaked off to visit his dear, dead children.

Of course, he never visited them with Mabel. No. He couldn't go with Mabel or Simon because he refused to let them see him cry, and cry he did, every time he visited the graves of his departed darlings.

How he missed little Felicity's musical laughter. And how he missed his tiny partner, Junior, his little shadow...

Of course, there would be no more visiting his children, because on a foolish whim, Bruce had purchased the map and sold his farm.

Against Mabel's wishes, no less.

But he'd insisted on it, and she had conceded, and he had sold his farm, along with the graves of his children, and brought his wife and living child here to this place, where any or all of them might end up being tossed over the side of the boulders to rot in the sun.

What a fool he'd been, what a tremendous fool.

The map had clearly been a counterfeit. Mabel had known that all along. Why hadn't he?

Because he'd wanted so badly for it to be real, wanted so badly for the map to provide a new life;, a life that would wipe away the pain and secret tears, a life that would give his family a fresh, happy start.

He'd allowed that possibility to blind him to the obvious facts, a mistake that still might prove fatal.

But now he was seeing things clearly.

Now, he understood not only his colossal mistake but also that it didn't matter where he was buried or if he was buried at all.

Death was final, at least for the flesh. What happened to his body afterward was inconsequential.

What really mattered was how one lived. And Bruce Duncan was determined to live the rest of his life, whether that amounted to one hour or sixty years, with his eyes fixed firmly on reality.

He resolved no matter what to do his best to set things right for his family and thereby redeem himself.

And that meant he had something else to do. Something he'd never done before.

But first, this.

"How will we get him over?" he asked Heck.

"We'll wait till dark," Heck said. "We'll lift him up to the bench and then carry him across the boulder tops as far as we can. Whoever's on guard duty up top won't want him to be too close."

Bruce admired Heck. His clear thinking, his toughness, his selflessness.

He'd never met a bigger man, not in size or spirit, and he counted himself lucky for having spent time with him. If he made it out of here, he knew he would spend the rest of his life telling stories of Heck's strength, intelligence, and bravery—not to mention the way he'd come all this distance to save Bruce's family.

Of course, Bruce hadn't always seen these things.

He hadn't respected Heck. He'd resented him. Resented him because Heck represented the truth when Bruce had wanted to keep a lie alive, the very lie that had landed him, his family, and Heck in this terrible situation.

Bruce felt a lump in his throat but tamped it down as he had so very many times since the children had passed, and when Heck was ready to move the body, Bruce stepped forward and grabbed Pete Twill's boots, and they carried their gruesome cargo across the enclosure away from the water and the living.

"Wish we could get him over this side," Heck said, pointing to the north-facing boulders on the opposite side of the enclosure from Cody's bench and the upper guard post.

"Maybe we can," Bruce said. "I'll try to get a rope to stick up there. Come nightfall, we might be able to climb up and hoist the body over. But first, I want to go talk to my wife."

"Good man," Heck said, clapping him on the shoulder. "I'm sure she's wondering what's been going on down here."

After the skirmish, Mabel had volunteered to go back up to the upper watch, allowing Clarence to rejoin the men and discuss matters. She'd taken Simon with her to shield him from the worst of this.

Thinking of her quiet strength, Bruce's heart swelled with pride and love.

Bruce parted ways with Heck and started for the rope ladder.

Pipher was down on all fours, gathering the food he'd dropped and piling it in plain sight.

Cody was sitting beside Becky with an arm over her shoulders.

The Count had retreated into the gloom, where he and his wife held their weird vigil against the back wall.

Strange, Bruce thought, *I surrendered my life to chase gold, but now, with gold right here, I don't even feel curious.*

Bruce scaled the rope ladder then ascended to the top, where his family clustered in the hollow beneath the rimrock, cuddled together like a single thing, like his very heart within his chest.

How he loved them.

"Hi, Pa!" Simon chimed.

"Hello, Bruce," Mabel said without smiling. She'd been cooler lately, and no surprise, given their situation and the mistakes he'd made that had landed them here.

Cooler, but not cold.

Or so he hoped.

Now, it was time to do that thing he'd never done before.

CHAPTER 34

Bruce tousled his son's hair and sent the boy back down to the pool, telling him to ask Heck if he needed any help.

"I heard shouting," Mabel said once the boy had left. "What happened down there?"

Bruce shook his head. "Might be easier to say what didn't happen. The heat's getting to people. And Pete Twill is dead."

Mabel nodded. Her expression hadn't changed, and though she talked to him, her eyes still scanned the surrounding country.

His wife. His wonderful, reliable wife.

Briefly, he told her everything that happened.

Mabel shook her head. "That Count is a horrible man. Possibly even worse than Pipher."

"Yes, at least Pipher doesn't hide his nature. The Count had me fooled for a while there. Speaking of which," he reached out and took her hand. "Mabel, I'm sorry. I've been a fool."

"What do you mean?" For just an instant, she flicked her

gaze toward his face. He saw the surprise there, which was understandable. After all, he was not accustomed to second guessing himself, let alone calling himself a fool.

But the time had come not only to recognize the truth but also to speak it.

"Buying the map, selling the farm, dragging you all the way out here," he said, "it was all foolishness. You tried to tell me in your gentle way, but I plowed right over your objections. I'm sorry, Mabel. I'm sorry I didn't listen to you, and I'm sorry I got us into this mess."

The faintest of smiles lifted the corners of her mouth. "Apology accepted, Bruce. Thank you for saying those things."

But he wasn't finished yet. "I can see everything clearly now. Heck Martin was only trying to save us from the start. I was just so determined to—"

And suddenly, that lump was back. He pushed it down again. Or rather, he tried to push it down—and failed.

The lump stuck, choking him with emotion, and the next thing he knew, he was crying, crying in front of his wife, and flooded with shame.

Mabel said nothing and held his hand as he wept, wept for his mistakes, wept for the damage he'd done, and most of all, wept for his dead children.

"I miss them so much," he cried. "So much. Sometimes, I think I can't take it."

"You can take it, Bruce," Mabel said, her voice soft and comforting as she continued to scan the countryside. "You have to take it. For Simon and for me. And you will. You are a strong man."

Where had she found such staggering strength? Had it always been inside her, waiting for this moment?

Yes, he thought, and was sure of the answer, certain that this inner strength had always been there and that he had, in his singlemindedness, failed to recognize it.

"I don't feel strong," he confessed, "not crying like this."

"It's long past time for you to cry, my love. Those babies, they were our hearts. But they're in heaven now, so we don't have to keep crying for them. Once, yes. Of course, once. It's unnatural not to mourn. And by mourn, I mean mourn together."

She glanced quickly toward him again, and he was certain that she knew everything, certain she understood his pain, his long suffering, and yes, the many tears he'd shed in private. She'd just loved him too much and known him too well to ask about it, understanding that to do so would have, at that time, belittled him.

"Thank you for staying strong," Bruce said. "I needed you, Mabel. I've been needing you, and I still need you."

"I know," she said, and there was that faint smile again. She gave his hand a squeeze. "I couldn't have hoped for a better husband or a more loving father to my children. Thank you for your kind words, Bruce, and for humbling yourself enough to mourn with me at last."

He nodded. His tears were over now. And somehow their shedding had soothed him far more than all the many tears he had shed in solitude.

"I'm back now, Mabel," he said. "I'm strong again. And I have moved past my foolishness. I can't repeat the past, but I promise I'll do whatever I can to get us out of this mess and start again."

"I know you will, Bruce. You're a good man, a good husband, and a good father. I know you will. We need to listen to Heck Martin."

"Yes," he said, nodding even though she wasn't looking his way. "We do. I recognize that now. If there's one person who will get us out of this, it's Heck. But Mabel?"

"Yes?"

"He's not the only person I'm going to listen to from now on. I'm going to listen to you, too, like I should have all along. Together, we'll get out of this and make a new life for our boy."

CHAPTER 35

"Come on," Heck said, crouching. "Climb up."

"Here goes," Bruce said and climbed up Heck's back onto his shoulders.

Once Bruce was firmly in place, Heck stood and walked over and scaled the rocks they'd piled at the base of the wall, lifting Bruce a few more feet into the air.

"How's that?" Heck asked, steadying his feet.

"Good," Bruce said. "My hands reach halfway up the boulder. "Can I have the rock, Becky?"

"Sure, Bruce," Becky said. "Here you go."

"Thank you," Bruce said. "All right. Here goes. On three. One, two, three…"

Heck felt the man lean back and snap forward as he threw the rock, and heard the other men grunt with effort, throwing the rope in the air so that it might chase after the rock to which it was tied.

The rock clattered back down followed by the length of skinny rope they'd borrowed from Clarence's rig.

"Close," Bruce said. "Might take a few tries."

In the end, it took more than a few tries. It took a few dozen. But they didn't quit, and eventually, the rock lodged in place.

Heck lowered Bruce to the ground. "Good work, men. Now, let's test it."

"Can I try?" Simon asked.

"Good idea," Heck said. "We'll start with the lightest."

Bruce held his son up, while Simon grabbed the rope and leaned back for all he was worth. When it held, Bruce released the boy and let him lean back, putting his full weight against the rope.

"My turn," Cody said, and a moment later, the young man was scaling the boulder, hand over hand.

The rope held, and Heck said a prayer of thanks when Cody reached the top.

"You ain't gonna believe this," Cody said, grinning down at them.

"What is it?"

"It's real flat up here, and the top of the rock kind of slopes upward at the front. Fella could lay up here with a rifle and be completely safe from folks down on the ground."

"That's great news," Heck said. "If they try to get in close again, we'll have a surprise for them."

"Sounds good to me, Heck. I'll tie off this rope and make sure it's secure."

"Good," Heck said, "but this does change one thing."

"What's that?"

"If we're gonna post somebody up there, we'll need a new spot for the body."

Heck climbed up to take a look.

The top of the boulder created a natural basin nothing short of ideal, with space enough for several people to hunker down behind the front of the stone, which jutted up a few feet in a natural wall.

By leaning to the right, Heck could peer out between the boulders at the baked scrubland beyond without making himself visible.

The only trouble was the sun. It broiled overhead, and it was far too hot to position a regular sentry atop this spot.

But once the sun wheeled to the west, the ridge behind them would cast its shadow over this spot, making it bearable.

The ridge...

A Sioux warrior positioned on that same ridge could hammer the position from above. It would be a long shot at a sharp angle, but the sentry would be completely vulnerable.

With that in mind, they could risk posting someone here at night but not in the daytime.

In the event of a sudden attack, someone could climb the rope in place and defend the northern side. Of course, the Sioux might coordinate an attack with someone on that ridge...

It was a lot to think about. The notion of a sniper camping out on the ridge troubled Heck.

In fact, it made his skin crawl just thinking about it, seeing as he was out in the open here.

The fact that no one took a shot pretty much proved that the Indians weren't positioned on the ridge... yet.

They likely came and went, but it would be mighty hot up there this time of day. Mighty hot, indeed.

Still, if the Sioux hadn't positioned a man up there yet, they likely would soon.

If only there was a way to know…

They talked through these things as they hoisted Pete Twill's body up onto the top of the boulder.

Once darkness fell, they could drag Twill along the tops of the boulders and pitch him over halfway to the front of the enclosure.

Cody seemed a little rattled, helping with the body, and Bruce looked disturbed but determined.

For Heck, it was not a particularly somber moment.

Pete Twill had been a bad person, cowardly and unreliable, the sort of person you could rely on only to let you down when you most needed him.

Not long ago, Twill had abandoned his post, and that desertion had resulted in the death of half a dozen good men.

Sure, every man had a soul, and you hoped, while they were alive, that they would mend their ways and come to Jesus, but ultimately, that was between every man and his maker and nobody else, and for Twill, it was too late to change anything.

If he'd made peace with the Lord, he was in a better place now. If not, he was in a far hotter place, wishing he could return to screaming in pain here upon the Earth.

Whichever way things shook out for him, they could do nothing to change that now.

So no, Heck didn't feel bad.

Whatever Pete Twill had been in life, this was just the shell.

Not good, not bad, not anything but a lifeless lump that weighed more than Heck would have expected.

It still looked like a man, of course, but...

"Wait a minute," Heck said, and his grin seemed to trouble the others. "Pete is still of use to us."

"Oh no," Cody said. "That's where I draw the line, Heck. I ain't no cannibal."

Heck laughed. "Neither am I Cody. And even if I were, I sure wouldn't want a filet of Pete."

Heck's joke turned Bruce green. The farmer raised his hands and shook his head.

"Sorry," Heck said. "It's just that I put two and two together. In life, Pete might have abandoned his brothers-in-arms, but we don't have to worry about him running now."

CHAPTER 36

"You're kidding," Becky said later, when Cody told her what they'd done with the body of Pete Twill. "Cody, that's positively ghoulish."

"Well, maybe a little, Becky, but it also might help keep us alive, so in my book, it's justified."

"I suppose." She gave a little shudder. "This is all so awful."

"You got that right. How are you holding up?"

"Okay, I guess. I mean, it's sad about Mr. Twill. Even if he wasn't the nicest fellow, he was someone."

"I suppose."

"What's that supposed to mean?"

"Means what I said. I suppose he was someone. Everybody's someone. But I'll be honest. From what I knew of Pete Twill, this is likely the most useful he's been to anybody in his whole life."

Becky frowned but said nothing.

"His buddy doesn't seem to be taking it too hard," Cody said, nodding to where Pipher crouched just inside the shade, sipping water, and looking out at the enclosure.

That's what the big deserter was still doing when a whooshing sound filled the air, and a dozen arrows rained down in the enclosure.

"Well, the joke's on them," Becky said, "because none of us was out in the open this time."

"I don't reckon they even cared about hitting us that time. Not really."

"What do you mean?"

"They're just messing with us. Keeping us on edge. It's like Heck says. They're trying to break our fighting spirit."

"How can they be so mean?"

Cody grinned at her question.

"Why in the world would you be smiling now, Cody?"

"Well, it's just I'd never thought of Indians as mean, exactly."

"Never thought of them as mean? Look at what they're doing. What did you think they were, charitable?"

"No, ma'am. Not hardly. But I don't know. I just didn't think of them as mean was all."

"What did you think of them as?"

"Just a fact of life, I suppose. Like heat and cold or a drought. Or rattlesnakes. They got their ways, and they're different from our ways. But yeah, I suppose when you think of them in our terms, they're a bunch of big ol' meanies."

She made a face at him. "Don't you go teasing me, Cody."

"I'm sorry. It just struck me funny was all."

"You're kind of peculiar."

That made him grin again. "I been called worse things."

"Cody?"

"Yeah?"

"Do you have anybody back in Texas?"

"Just my brothers and sisters, like I told you. Ma and Pa both—"

"No, I mean *somebody*. A girl."

"Oh," he said, and felt heat come into his face as he realized what she was asking. "No, ma'am. I ain't got nobody back there."

"Did you ever?"

"No, ma'am."

She looked away, trying and failing to hide a smile.

Now, why did that make her smile?

He didn't know, but for some strange reason, her confusing smile made him happy and gave him a little rush of excitement.

"How about you?" he asked.

"What about me?" she asked, peeking at him over her shoulder.

"You got somebody waiting on you back home?"

"You think I'd set out for California if I did?"

He laughed. "Speaking of peculiar, you just asked me the same question, knowing full and well that I set out from Texas."

"Fair enough. The answer is no. And before you ask, the other answer is no, too."

"What other answer?"

"I never did have anybody."

He pushed his hat back and squinted at her, trying to see if she was putting him on.

"Why are you looking at me that way?" Becky asked. "I know I look a sight but—"

"I'm just trying to see if you're putting me on is all. You must be. How could a girl so beautiful as you not have a bunch of men lined up, offering her the world?"

Becky laughed and turned bright red. "Don't tease me, Cody."

"I ain't teasing you, Becky. I wouldn't never tease you about that. You're the most beautiful girl I ever seen."

"Pshaw! Now I've heard everything." She said this in a complaining, disbelieving tone, but he could see it pleased her.

When she turned to him again, she said, "Cody, I'm gonna ask you something, and I want you to tell me the truth, okay?"

"All right. Ask."

"Not yet."

"All right. When you gonna ask?"

"Well, I just want to make sure is all."

"Make sure of what?"

"That you understand."

"Understand what?"

"I'm trying to tell you, but you keep interrupting me," she laughed.

"Sorry, darling. You go ahead."

Her face brightened again. "Darling?"

"Sorry. I'm from Texas."

"So you say that to all the girls?"

Cody laughed. "No, ma'am, you're the first. But I've heard other men call girls that."

"Well, it's okay. I don't mind, actually. It sounds kind of sweet. But what I'm trying to ask you, well, I don't want you to feel like you gotta say yes."

"All right. I won't."

"You won't say yes?"

He laughed. "I won't feel like I gotta say yes."

"All right. Because it's a big deal, and I don't want you feeling like you gotta do something just to be nice and then end up resenting me."

"You sure know how to string a fella along, Becky. Go on and ask me."

"If we live through this, will you take me back to Pennsylvania?"

"Yes, ma'am, I will. I'll take you home to your family."

Becky sighed. "Thank you, Cody," she said, and slipped her hand into his. "That means an awful lot to me."

They just sat there then, holding hands. Cody was very happy. He didn't know what to say and didn't need to say anything anyway. It was enough to just sit there, feeling her hand in his.

They were still sitting there, holding hands, when a gunshot rang out overhead.

CHAPTER 37

Though it wouldn't have seemed possible, the day grew even hotter than the days before, so blisteringly hot, in fact, that the survivors barely moved within the shadows.

They were tired and hungry and thirsty, but mostly, they were hot.

This, Heck knew, presented yet another advantage to their adversaries, who would not have as much shade but would hold up far better under the torturous conditions.

"Clarence, keep an eye on the ridge," Heck called across the enclosure. "In three minutes, I'm going to run to you."

Heck wasn't worried about announcing his intentions. Even if the sniper understood English, he wouldn't be able to hear Heck's words all the way up there.

"Don't do it," Clarence called back.

"Have to. They might rush you, try to get us to help you and come out into the open. Besides, I want to draw out the shooter. Keep an eye on that ridge."

"Will do. That was a good idea with Twill."

"Yeah, he served his purpose well. Now we know beyond any shred of doubt that they have a sniper on that ridge."

They had stretched Twill's corpse out like a sentry atop the rock.

The decoy had worked. A sniper had fired three times from high above, killing a dead man and announcing his position.

"Only one up there, you reckon?"

"Sounded that way to me. You?"

"Only one was shooting, but maybe there are others up there, waiting for more targets."

"Maybe. We'll see in a minute here."

"You sure about this, Heck?"

"I'm sure. Stay ready."

They were quiet for a time, letting the watcher above think their conversation was over.

When Heck moved, he moved fast, sprinting across the enclosure and zigzagging like his life depended on it, which it very much did.

A gunshot cracked high above, and a round kicked up dust just in front of Heck.

That was close, Heck thought, reaching the passage and the safety of the sheltering rocks. *What a shot.*

Clarence returned fire. "I saw him," Clarence said. "He's way up there near the top. See that shelf of darker rock jutting out? He's just to the left of that."

"Good to know," Heck said. "Man, can he shoot."

"You're a fool, charging out here."

"It was a measured risk. Besides, I can't leave you alone out here."

They moved forward to where they could see out the front of the passage in case the Sioux launched an attack.

"This sniper's a problem," Clarence said.

"Yes, he is. It changes things."

"Water's running low, too."

"And the food. Not just for us, either. Horses have cropped the forage to stubble."

"We're running out of time, Heck."

"Yes, we are. Something's gotta give. I was hoping people might come from Hope City, but we can't rely on them. We have to extricate ourselves."

"Extricate? Does that mean get ourselves out of here?"

"Correct."

"Well, then I concur. We need to extricate ourselves before we run out of water or nerve. Question is, how we gonna do that?"

"We gotta strike back."

"I like the thought, but how are we gonna do that? Who would we even attack? They're shooting at us from four different directions. Far as I can tell, they split up pretty good."

"That's good. Fewer people to fight."

"Yeah, but how do you find them? And who do you go after? And how do you keep them from shooting you when you attack?"

"You ask a lot of questions, my friend."

"I've found asking questions helps keep me alive."

"There you go again, thinking about survival."

"Somebody's got to, especially when our leader starts talking about making a charge."

"Not a charge. We gotta be stealthy."

"I'm just waiting to hear the rest of it."

"Well, we gotta take out the sniper first."

"Long shot. I might be able to make it if he'd be so kind as to come out into the open, but how are we gonna get him to do that?"

"We aren't," Heck said. "I'm going up there tonight to kill him."

"Risky."

"No riskier than sitting tight. Like I said, something's gotta give."

"You're right about that. But how do you propose to get up there?"

"I'll climb it. Gotta go slow, stay silent. He hears me, I'll be a sitting duck. I'm gonna try to kill him silently, too."

"Killing ain't generally all that silent."

"No, but for my plan to work, it's gotta be silent. See, if he's up there, the rest of the plan won't work. It won't work with a sniper watching for us, and it won't work if I make a bunch of noise and stir up the rest of the Sioux."

"And what would the rest of this plan be?"

"Sneaking out there a few hundred yards and hitting them hard."

"You do understand that's crazy, don't you?"

Heck spread his hands. "We've got to do it, Clarence."

"We?"

Heck nodded. "I'm hoping you'll come with me."

Clarence frowned, stared at the ground for a few seconds, then nodded. "I try not to do foolish things—avoiding them helps me to stay alive—but yeah, I'll go with you."

"Good man. I'm gonna ask Cody, too."

"He'll do."

"Yeah, the boy has sand."

"Which group are we attacking? You got some to the north, some to the south, and some straight out ahead of us to the east."

"We'll go straight ahead."

"You sound pretty sure of that."

"I am. That's where their water is. I reckon they're set up out by where they burned the Duncans' wagon. I'm guessing they moved the Count's water barrels up to that position. It's close but not too close. Otherwise, they would have had to have moved all of those heavy water barrels, including the Duncans', someplace else, and we've given them no reason to go to all that work, especially in this heat."

Clarence grinned. "You might be onto something."

The men were pleased to have a plan, and they fell into semi-contented silence, enduring the heat and waiting for dark.

But before darkness arrived, gunshots cracked from dead ahead, and a raiding party came rushing straight at them.

CHAPTER 38

"Riders coming!" Heck shouted to those in the enclosure. "Stay back! They're trying to draw you into the sniper's line of fire."

Heck and Clarence fired at the charging warriors, unseating two riders.

The warriors broke off their charge and returned fire from a hundred yards out while two men dismounted and disappeared into the scrub.

Heck and Clarence fired again.

Heck's shot hit home and unseated another rider, but Clarence caught a ricochet as he was firing, and his shot went astray.

The Sioux rode off, save for their dead and the two men hiding on the ground a hundred yards out.

"You hit bad?" Heck asked.

"Just bad enough to make me miss," Clarence grumbled. "Burned me across the back. Ever hear of such a thing?

They're right in front of us, and they shoot me in the back."

Clarence's shirt was dark with blood across the shoulders.

"Take off that shirt," Heck said, "and I'll have a look at the wound."

"All right, but it can wait. You see those boys drop onto the ground out there?"

"I did."

"Reckon they're gathering their dead?"

"I do."

"Well, then, we can wait on my wound. Soon as I see one of those bodies move, I'm shooting."

"Don't."

Clarence looked at him like he was crazy. "You gonna let them take the bodies?"

Heck nodded.

"Why are you so charitable all of a sudden?"

"Because they're gonna get those bodies sooner or later. It's their way."

"Ah," Clarence said, nodding. "So if we don't let them have them now, they'll come back at night."

"Exactly."

"And you don't want to have to wonder if they're out there when we make our counterattack."

"Right again. Let's have a look at that bullet wound."

Clarence pulled off his shirt, and Heck winced—not at the sight of wound but at Clarence's horribly scarred back.

Heck, who was no stranger to scars, had never seen anything like it.

"How's it look?" Clarence asked.

"Not bad," Heck said, picking a bit of shirt fabric from the wound. "Wish I had a way to clean it out, but I think you'll be all right."

"Figured," Clarence said and pulled his shirt back over his muscular, impossibly scarred torso. "So now's when you ask me how I got the scars."

"You get whipped?"

"Yes, sir. That's exactly what happened."

"You were a slave?"

"Born and raised."

"How did you escape?"

"I didn't. They set me free. My owner was a good man. Treated my family right. Treated everybody right, as far as I could tell. I worked hard for him. Got to be friends. I know that probably sounds impossible, but it's true. He even broke the law, teaching me to read."

"So why would he whip you?"

"He didn't. His son did."

"The father let him?"

"No, the father was dead."

"Oh."

"Mr. Harrington's son, Chad, hated me because I was so close to his father. Mr. Harrington knew that and protected me."

"He should've cut you loose."

"I know. Believe me, I know. But I don't think he could bear the thought of losing his best friend. Especially not because he'd been sick for a while."

Heck nodded.

"But then Mr. Harrington got real sick," Clarence said, and

Heck could see the memory saddened him. "He knew he was gonna die, just like he knew what would happen to me if I hung around, so he set things up for me to go free. Trouble is, his son knew what he'd done. So when Mr. Harrison died, before the will was even read, Chad whipped me to within an inch of my life."

"Why didn't he finish the job?"

"Folks knew Mr. Harrington liked me. They would have frowned on Chad killing me. Besides, I expect he was confident I'd die with how bad he'd laid me open."

"How did you survive?"

"Stubbornness, friends, the grace of God. I needed all of it to pull through. After Chad worked me over, he dumped me outside the gate and told me to enjoy my freedom. At least that's what folks said he told me. I was unconscious by then."

"I imagine."

Clarence nodded, his eyes going temporarily vacant with memory. "Here's the funny thing. I spent the next two months right under Chad's nose, and he didn't even know it. Friends took me in, hid me, nursed me back to health. The whole time I was living on Chad's property and eating his food."

"Man, that would have burned him if he'd known."

"It did burn him."

"He found out?"

"Sure. I told him… right before I killed him."

The confession surprised Heck. Surprised him but didn't put him off. "How'd you do it?"

"Got an ax, waited till he was alone in the house, then went in and took care of business. I thought about whipping him like he'd whipped me, but in the end, it wasn't so much about revenge as it was stopping him from hurting other folks."

"And then you ran?"

"And then I ran."

"How long ago was that?"

"Fourteen years. Almost fifteen. The West has been good to me, Heck. People out here, most of them have that big frontier spirit. They don't care so much about names or titles or the color or your skin. They judge you by what sort of man you are."

"It's the way things should be."

"Yes, it is. So let's be careful killing Indians tonight. I'd like to keep on enjoying the West if it's all the same to you."

"Sounds like a plan, my friend. Sounds like a very good plan."

CHAPTER 39

C ount Viktor Karpov sat with his back to the wall, feeling
trapped.

Beside him Natalia drowsed in the unbearable heat.

Of course, it wasn't just the heat. It was thirst and hunger
and pressure, too. Natalia was a strong woman, but even she
had her limits.

And him? Was he approaching a limit?

No.

Despite all these things, despite the looming threat of Pipher
and the Indians, and the stinging humiliation he had suffered at
the hands of Heck Martin, he would endure.

This was not his life. His life was west of here in California.

Far from this place, far from Heck Martin and everyone
who had witnessed Viktor's undoing.

In California, he would start over and make a new life, a
worthy life.

Nothing had changed.

Well, except for Becky. He would no longer be taking her along.

But that was simple enough to fix. He would acquire a Spanish mistress instead. One with good breeding, one who would give him black-haired babies that he could take with him on his triumphant return to Russia.

He would present these black-haired, black-eyed heirs to his father, proving the General had been wrong all along, about everything, and most importantly, about Viktor.

Yes, that was his future.

But to reach it, he must endure. Endure, survive, and leave this place with the gems.

He glanced across the pools at Pipher, who sat alone, drowsing, near the edge of the shade.

It would be easy to pick up his Enfield, sight down its long barrel, and smash the thief's head like a rotten pumpkin.

But these fools wouldn't stand for it.

Viktor had been so close. He'd had them ready to execute Pipher, which would have made his life much easier, but then Heck Martin had stepped in and ruined everything.

It made no sense. Why did they listen to Heck? He was nothing. He did not come from a great family and apparently had no formal education.

So why did they listen to him? Especially when he stood in direct opposition to Viktor. Why?

It must be his height. That was the only possibility that made sense. It must be Heck's freakish height that won their confidence.

Which made a degree of sense. Peter the Great had been six

feet, eight inches tall, after all, and look at all he had accomplished.

So yes, it must be Heck's height swaying people.

For a moment, when shooting broke out at the front of the enclosure, Viktor had hoped Heck Martin might be killed. Unfortunately, Heck had survived and driven off the savages, deflating Viktor's other hope as well.

He wanted to fight.

He wanted to have at these savages, wanted them to rush the enclosure with reckless abandon so he could get up on the walls and cut them down like a scythe cutting wheat.

It irked him that he had so far not had an opportunity to kill a savage. When he did, he would show these others how a real man fought.

His stomach growled. Absentmindedly, he plucked a piece of jerky from his shirt pocket and nibbled at it while continuing to analyze the situation.

For as much as he loathed Pipher, the brute was a temporary problem. The bigger problem was Heck Martin.

Heck had publicly belittled Viktor, and for that, he deserved to die, but that's not what made him such a problem.

These people liked Heck, listened to him, stood up for him. That stole Viktor's power.

But a bigger problem lurked on the horizon, waiting for him to escape this dreadful place.

Heck Martin wasn't just tall and bold. He ran a trading post and talked to people heading east and west along the Oregon Trail. Apparently, he'd even started some backwater town.

Heck was exactly the sort of man that this miserable country celebrated and elevated, exactly the sort of man who would invariably rise to prominence, exactly the sort of man who could destroy Viktor's reputation in America, ruining him and forcing him to go back to the General worse off than before, penniless, defeated, and disgraced.

Then, shortly after darkness fell, Viktor's nemesis came back from guard duty and shared his foolish plan to scale the mountain, take out the sniper, and then lead an assault on the savages' main position.

It was madness. Absolute insanity. Suicide.

But that didn't stop Clarence or Cody from volunteering to join the wildly stupid assault.

The heat must be getting to them, Viktor thought. The heat, thirst, and pressure.

That was where his breeding showed. He wasn't like them. He wouldn't break under the pressure. He wouldn't throw his life away on some foolish foray just because he was tired of waiting.

He would remain clear in his thinking and decisive in his actions.

His stomach grumbled again. Once more, he dipped his fingers into his shirt pocket—and was shocked to find it empty.

He'd already eaten the last of his food?

The realization shocked him. His stomach growled in protest.

Natalia would still have food. But it wouldn't be enough. What would he eat after finishing his wife's food?

Panic rose in him. He and Natalia had to get out of this place, had to get to safety and food and water. If they stayed here, they would all die.

And then, suddenly, he had it.

Heck Martin's trip up the mountain…

If, against all odds, Heck managed to kill the savage, it would create an opening in the enemy lines.

An opening he and Natalia could exploit. All they needed to do was ride out of here.

But they couldn't leave as soon as Heck killed the savage. If they tried, the others would stop them.

The thing to do was to wait for Heck and the idiots to attack the Indians.

Then, with all of those who might stop him fighting and dying, he and Natalia could take the box, get their horses, and run.

The only possible obstacle would be Pipher. The big soldier was cunning with the instincts of a scavenger.

Pipher might be having similar thoughts.

In fact, he was staring at Viktor now. Staring and smiling.

Pipher might very well attempt to steal the box at that same moment, steal it and ride west.

Well, then, Viktor would just have to shoot Pipher shortly after Heck and his men left.

Content with his plan but knowing he would need his strength, Viktor closed his eyes and allowed himself to relax, and a short time later, he was snoring softly beside his slumbering wife.

CHAPTER 40

Heck knelt beside the pool, dribbling a bit of its precious, dwindling water into the dirt and stirring it in.

"What are you doing, Mr. Martin?" Simon Duncan's tiny voice asked.

His parents were talking a short distance away.

"Making a mask," Heck said, grinning at the boy.

"A mask?"

"That's right. A mud mask." Heck demonstrated, scooping up some mud and smearing it onto his face. "This way, I'll be harder to see in the darkness."

"Oh," the boy said, clearly impressed. "Can I do it, too?"

"Not yet, Simon. We don't have enough water to play games, but I'll tell you what. Once we get back to Hope City, I'll let you cover yourself head to toe in mud."

The boy was all smiles then.

As Heck was finishing his camouflage, Bruce and Mabel Duncan came walking over.

"I'd like to go with you tonight," Bruce said.

"Thanks, Bruce. But this is a one-man job."

"No, I mean later. I want to go with you and Cody and Clarence."

"Oh," Heck said. He glanced at Mabel. If she had any fear, she wasn't letting it show. "It's gonna be dangerous."

"I know," Bruce said. "I'm going. Like you said, maybe if we hit them hard enough, they'll decide to try their luck elsewhere."

Heck noticed that Simon was beaming now, staring at his father in admiration.

"All right," Heck said, hoping he wasn't making a mistake. "We'll be lucky to have you along, Bruce."

He held out his hand, and they shook.

"I'm guessing we should cover our faces, too?" Bruce asked.

"That's right. Be ready when I come back. We won't tarry. Once the sniper is gone, we gotta strike fast and hard. That's the only shot we got at making them turn tail."

Clarence and Cody shook Heck's hand and wished him luck and told him to be careful.

Sergeant Gentry, who had managed to get up the boulder despite his wounded leg, called down with similar sentiments from the upper post.

And then Heck took a last drink of water, climbed the rope up the northern side, and crawled over the boulders to where they met the cliff.

A mantle of clouds had slid over the valley like a lid atop a coffin.

Luckily, this made the night very dark.

Unfortunately, the mantle of clouds also trapped the day's

heat, giving no relief, and making Heck's hands sweaty as he began his high-risk climb.

To avoid making noise, he left his canteen and rifle behind, and he'd tied down the head of his tomahawk so it wouldn't knock into the cliff.

He also carried his Bowie knife and his Colt, though he would only use the revolver if everything went terribly wrong.

Slowly, he climbed, glad he'd thought to swap out his boots for moccasins. The moccasins were quieter than boots and allowed him to feel the surface of the cliff beneath his toes.

He took his time, testing every fingerhold and toehold, and moved slowly to avoid making noise.

The first portion of the climb was very steep, and he had to start and stop several times, working his way from side to side until he'd found a way up.

Twice, his sweat-slick fingers slipped on the rock, and he nearly fell, but both times, he managed to hug the cliffside and avoid death.

Because from this height, any fall would certainly result in death.

After a long, exhausting, and excruciatingly slow climb lasting perhaps two hours, he finally reached the top of the ridge, having climbed to the northern end, on the opposite side of the protruding rock formation from where Clarence had spotted the sniper.

Heck paused there, sweating profusely, his muscles trembling with exertion.

His mind protested, telling him to get up and finish the job, but his body needed rest.

He'd been going hard for a long time, running on too little sleep and not nearly enough food or water.

So he lay there, breathing softly, resting, and listening.

The night was silent as death and hot as Hades.

Despite that heat, however, Heck realized he was no longer sweating. His skin was hot and dry, and he knew that he was dehydrated.

With this thought, he rose. He couldn't afford to lay there, getting drier by the moment, and then cramp when he needed his muscles the most.

He unsheathed his Bowie, put it in his teeth like a pirate, and moved across the ridge on hands and knees. He would be harder to see if he crawled on his body, he knew, but this was quieter and quicker, and he needed to hurry, needed to finish this job with plenty of time left to raid the Indians.

If he took too long here and couldn't make the second attack, the Sioux would simply replace the sniper, and Heck and the others would never have such a chance again.

It was now or never.

So he crawled forward, knife gripped tightly in his teeth.

Reaching the peak, he stopped and flattened himself against the ground and peered over the edge.

It was a dizzying drop to Petit Wells. The Indian who'd hit Pete Twill's corpse must be one incredible shot.

That's probably why they posted him here, Heck realized. He was probably their top shot.

Where are you? he thought, scanning the gloom.

He moved forward a few feet, sweeping his gaze over the scrubby slope.

Had the sniper cleared out with darkness? Had he retreated to—

No.

There he was, on a little outcropping of rock thirty feet away and fifteen feet down the cliffside, sitting with his back against the stone.

Heck scanned the area carefully and saw only the lone figure.

Was he asleep?

No, he shifted.

Heck quickly looked away. Some people—and especially Indians—could feel it when you stared at them.

When he looked back, the man was sitting there, still as a stone again.

Heck watched, waited, listened.

Everything was still save for a slight breeze out of the west.

It was the first breeze he'd felt in a long time, and under different circumstances, he would have welcomed it, appreciating the small relief it offered, interrupting the torturous sameness of the hot, still air.

But now, in this moment, the breeze froze his heart with trepidation.

Quickly, he untied his tomahawk and stood.

The sniper's head bobbed up and down like a dog scenting the air. And that's just what he was doing, scenting the breeze, smelling Heck.

Heck rushed forward as silently as he could.

The man stood and turned, saw Heck, and started to lift his rifle when Heck's whirling tomahawk hit him square in the face.

The man dropped to the ground and slid several feet downslope, dislodging a clattering cascade of pebbly scree that sounded like an avalanche to Heck, thanks to his nearness and heightened senses but probably couldn't be heard from any distance whatsoever.

Then, all was still and silent again, save for that tickling breeze that had almost cost Heck his life.

He said a prayer of thanks. It had been a desperate throw, and he was lucky to have killed his man.

He was also thankful for the Sioux culture's practice of silence.

A white man would have cried out in alarm.

Heck considered these things as he made his way down the embankment, retrieved the man's rifle, and searched the corpse and bench for valuables, coming away with two canteens, a nice knife, and a good deal of shot and powder.

There was also a sack of jerky, several biscuits, and a roll of thin corn cakes.

Heck ate a little of each and washed it down with a good amount of water, then ate some more.

Yes, he would share some of this bounty with those down below, but he had earned this share.

Besides, he needed food and drink because he'd expended a lot of energy coming up here.

And the night was just beginning.

CHAPTER 41

T he guy had guts.

Pipher had to give Heck that much credit when he came back with a rifle and food and the news that he'd taken out the sniper and thereby opened the westward way.

But then again, a lot of stupid people had guts. Sometimes, they got lucky. Sometimes, they got killed.

Heck had gotten lucky.

Now, he and the other three nincompoops were slipping past Pipher, who stood watch at the front of the passage, and heading out into the darkness to take the fight to the Indians.

"Good luck, you boys," Pipher said, grinning to himself. "Go get 'em."

He waited another ten minutes, making sure they didn't come to their senses, change their minds, and run back into the enclosure.

But no. They did not return. Apparently, they were committed to the cause.

Just like Pipher was committed to his.

Within the enclosure, all was silent.

Sergeant Gentry was up top, standing a long watch rather than coming back down with his bad leg. By serving extra shifts, he was also allowing the others to rest.

That was mighty nice of the good sergeant. And mighty convenient for Pipher, who abandoned his post and marched straight back to the wells, where Becky and Mrs. Duncan were huddled near a small fire, clearly nervous for their men.

The boy lay further back, sleeping hard.

Even further back, the Count and Countess lay near the gold.

"Mr. Pipher," Mabel Duncan said, clearly surprised to see him, "is everything all right?"

"Peachy keen, ma'am," he said, walking past her. "Never better."

"But you've abandoned your post," Becky remarked. "What if the Indians attack?"

Pipher ignored the women, went straight to the Count, and kicked the sleeping man in the leg.

The Count spoke rapidly in Russian, sat up, and reached for his revolver.

"Don't even think about it," Pipher said, pointing his rifle at him. "Hands up. And you keep your hands where I can see them, too, ma'am. I know about that little derringer of yours."

"What is the meaning of this?" the Count demanded, sounding haughtier than ever.

"Nobody try anything," Pipher said, raising his voice just enough so that the women could hear him, too, "or I'll kill all of you."

The Count glared at him.

Pipher chuckled. "Don't be cross, Count. Simplest thing would've been to just shoot you in your sleep. But I remember you standing up for me when they were gonna kill me. Of course, later, you said I should be killed. Hmm. What to do?"

He held his rifle on the Russian, who showed no fear, only anger.

"Aw, shucks," Pipher said. "I'm feeling pretty good, what with Heck opening the western way for me."

"You're leaving?" Becky asked.

"That's right, sugar plum. You want to come with me, live the high life?"

"No thank you."

"All right. Your loss. I'm getting out of here while the getting's good. And I'll be taking your gold with me, Count."

The Count spat a stream of barbed Russian that could only be curses.

"Good thing I don't talk that language, or I might take offense," Pipher said. "It's up to you. Either you give me the gold, or I kill you and take it anyway."

"It isn't gold, you idiot," the Count said. "It's gems."

"That'll do," Pipher said. "Get the box for me. After you give me your guns. First you, Count. Don't even think of turning that muzzle in my direction. Turn it the other way and set it down as far as you can reach. That's it. Your turn, Countess. Nice and easy."

He disarmed them then had the Count and Becky and Mrs. Duncan sit farther back, off to the left, while the Countess uncovered the box and brought it to him.

Then he sent her to join the others.

The boy slept through it all.

Which was good. Pipher had a soft spot for kids. He didn't want to scare the little tyke.

"Becky, round up the horses. Put the saddle on that big red stallion for me. I've been admiring that horse since I first laid eyes on him. I'll ride him and lead the others."

"You're taking all the horses?" Mrs. Duncan asked. "Why?"

"First, so none of you can follow me."

"Why would we?" the Count said. "You took our guns."

"But the other folks still have guns. I'm gonna have my hands full getting past the Injuns. I don't need to be watching my back trail for you, too."

"You should watch your back trail," the Count snarled.

"See, now, that's exactly the sort of talk that makes me think I might be better off just shooting you right now."

The Count said nothing more.

"The other reason I'm taking the horses," Pipher explained, feeling expansive in his big moment, "is to help me get away from these Injuns. I'm riding fast and quiet. Meanwhile, I'll stampede these horses. So any Injuns that come after me will have their hands full with them. They want these horses more than they want me."

Pipher told Mrs. Duncan to lash the gems to the stallion and had Natalia fill up the canteens and lash them to the horse, too.

"You can't take the canteens," Becky protested.

"I can, and I am."

"But we'll die," Mrs. Duncan said. "We'll never be able to ride out of here without water."

"Not my problem. Besides, you might get lucky. Maybe someone will come and rescue you."

He put everyone back against the wall then checked the saddle, box, and gear.

"What a fine horse this is," Pipher said. "Tell Heck Martin I'm much obliged."

He eased the stallion forward, trying to figure the best way to gather the other horses' leads, when the horses surprised him and simply followed Heck Martin's big red horse.

They were drawn to the stallion. He was their leader.

It surprised Pipher, who didn't know horses well and who'd never willingly followed a leader in all his life.

He was his own man, a stallion among geldings.

"Looks like these other horses agree," Pipher laughed. "Seems like they'll follow us straight out of here. I can tell this stallion's ready to run, too. Fine horse like this is meant to run. Ain't used to being cooped up."

Like me, he thought, climbing into the saddle. *I'm not meant to stay cooped up, either. I'm not meant for small things like this group or army life or any of the rest of it.*

The others watched him with bitter expressions.

"Why the long faces?" he called back, riding off, followed by the horses. "Aren't you happy for me? This is my lucky day."

CHAPTER 42

Heck crawled over the hard ground, moving silently through the darkness, followed by Clarence, Cody, and Bruce.

With exquisite slowness, they crossed the dusty land, inching toward the spot where the Sioux had burned the Duncans' wagon.

Heck stopped frequently, knowing the other men might be tiring. During these moments of rest, he scanned the darkness and listened hard.

Everything was still now. Still and silent, as if the whole world were holding its breath in anticipation.

He crawled farther, and they came to the charred ruins of the wagon.

They were close.

Very close.

Unless Heck's hunch about the water barrels was wrong.

From far behind them, behind even Petit Wells, came the screech of a hunting hawk.

But of course, hawks didn't screech like that at night.

Not real hawks.

That hadn't been a bird at all but a Sioux warrior, giving a signal.

The question was, a signal for what?

Had Heck just left the others open to the long-awaited attack?

Before he could even consider the repercussions, he heard snorting and the pounding of hooves, and a party of Sioux warriors came riding at them out of the darkness.

CHAPTER 43

As Heck was crawling out of the enclosure, Red pounded westward, followed by the other eight horses.

It felt good, running again. Red's big muscles warmed quickly, and his heart pounded with the joy of cutting through the night, hooves pounding the earth beneath him.

Atop him, Pipher grinned, feeling the horse's excitement.

What a horse. What a fine animal. This stallion would carry him all the way to California.

The only trouble was the other horses.

They were still following.

Didn't they understand they were free? Free to run and go where they pleased? Why wouldn't they go off and be useful to him?

As it was, they were the opposite of useful. They were running behind him, making a racket.

If there were any Indians out here...

He hunched low over the stallion and urged him forward. If the other horses insisted on following, he would just outpace them.

But then, abruptly, the stallion halted.

Pipher lurched forward with a grunt but managed to stay in the saddle.

What was the stupid beast doing, trying to get him killed?

The stallion turned its head and looked backward, apparently waiting for the other horses to catch up.

Pipher pulled the reins, forcing the stallion's head forward, and kicked him in the ribs, trying to get the stupid thing running again.

The horse just stood there and pulled its head back around, staring out their back trail.

Pipher quickly scanned the surrounding darkness. He could see nothing, of course.

All was silent, but that only increased the menace because in Indian territory, there was no solace in silence.

The other horses had nearly caught up.

Pipher, who had always been good at thinking on his feet, decided to wait for them. Then the stallion would run again.

But when the horses reached them, the stallion continued to stare back toward the enclosure.

That's when Pipher finally understood.

The stallion hadn't been waiting for the horses. He'd been looking for Heck Martin… and still was.

"Forget him," Pipher said in a snarled whisper. "You're my horse now. Let's go."

He yanked the stallion's head around and kicked him with his bootheels.

The horse ignored him.

Not far away, a hawk gave a long, shrill cry in the darkness.

Instantly, Pipher's flesh crawled with goosebumps.

He'd never heard a hawk at night.

"We're going this way, stupid," Pipher said and hauled even harder on the reins.

The stallion went reluctantly in that direction—and then kept going, spinning all the way back around to face Petit Wells, whipping about so quickly that Pipher nearly fell.

"Hey!" Pipher barked, momentarily forgetting his fear of the Indians. He cursed the horse, which was sprinting now, heading back toward the wells.

"Whoa!" Pipher struck the horse with a powerful blow to the neck. "Stop, you stupid horse!"

The stallion slammed to a stop.

Pipher's body kept moving and came out of the saddle. His chest crashed into the horse's neck, and he tried to grab hold.

Suddenly, the stallion reared, pounded back down, spun halfway around, and bucked Pipher into the air.

Pipher turned half a somersault in midair. Falling, he cursed, realizing he was in trouble.

He had always been agile with a good sense of the world around him. In a fight, he'd start ducking a punch before the other fella even threw it. And his body had the sense to shift its weight with the counterpunch that would clean the other guy's clock.

He was like a cat that way. Combined with his natural strength, it had always given him the winning edge.

But now, trapped in this fall, he could do nothing, only sense that he was falling at a bad angle, head down.

Then that angle met its end.

The back of Pipher's head slammed into the hard ground.

There was an explosion of pain, and darkness consumed him.

CHAPTER 44

Heck flattened himself on the ground, hoping the other men would follow suit.

Because fifty yards away, many warriors were streaming past.

Nine, he counted, *ten, eleven...*

Eleven warriors rushed away toward Petit Wells.

Was this it?

Were they attacking the enclosure?

There was nothing Heck could do about it now. He had to stick to the plan, had to make this foray count.

He crawled forward. To his relief, the others followed.

A short time later, he topped a small rise and looked down upon the Sioux camp.

Half a dozen warriors sat among the water barrels, talking quietly. They looked sleepy, and Heck assumed they'd been awakened when a sentry heard the hawk's cry.

A rifle lay close to each man.

Behind them were the spoils of war: heaps of food, sacks of grain for the horses, clothing, a sheet metal stove.

And farther back, horses and mules, more steeds than there were men. A dozen and a half at least.

As the others slid in beside Heck, he executed a deadly pantomime, pointing from himself to a specific warrior, then from each of the others to another enemy.

His friends nodded, understanding, and got their rifles into position.

When Heck fired, they all fired—and all hit their marks.

The surviving warriors grabbed for their rifles, but Heck had his pistol ready and shot one of them down as he was coming to his feet.

The other plunged away into darkness.

Heck jumped up and charged after him, calling to his friends, "Round up the horses."

Heck knew better than to charge straight after the Indian. Instead, he cut away at an angle, getting the high ground.

There was a bright flash of light in the darkness. The warrior's rifle boomed, and Heck lurched to one side with supernatural speed.

The bullet burned across his side in a line of fire, but there was no punch to it, no walloping impact, so he knew it had only grazed him.

He returned fire with the Colt.

The shadowy figure gave a cry and crumpled in the darkness.

Moving with great haste, Heck and the others looted the

camp. They didn't have the time or means to gather everything, but they took the horses and mules that hadn't run off, secured Indians' canteens and weapons and ammunition, and packed the saddle bags full of food.

At any second, the riders could return, but these actions were worth the risk. Without food and water, they would soon die.

Conversely, they were striking hard with this raid.

"Give me a hand, Cody," Heck said. "These barrels are only half full. Let's strap them onto the mules."

"They're gonna come back, Heck."

"Yeah, they are, so let's hurry. We gotta try. This water could mean the difference between life and death for us and them. Clarence, Bruce, you keep watch."

The Sioux were brave but seldom squandered their lives. The loss of these six warriors would affect them deeply.

As would the loss of the food and water. Especially the water.

At least a dozen warriors remained. Would these losses be enough to drive them away?

Everything depended on what was happening back at the enclosure, which is exactly where Heck and friends needed to return as quickly as possible.

"Don't hear any shooting back at the wells," Clarence pointed out, climbing onto the horse he'd chosen.

"You're right," Heck said. "That's good. Maybe even very good."

Why the hawk's cry, then? Where had the riders been going in such a hurry?

"We gotta get back there," Heck said.

The men nodded, their eyes bright with purpose and the excitement of combat.

And they rode for Petit Wells.

CHAPTER 45

Everything in Heck wanted to race straight to the enclosure, but he led them in a wide arc to the south before angling back toward the wells, wanting to avoid a head-on collision with the Sioux if they came charging back in response to the gunshots.

Despite the desperate situation, it felt good to be atop a horse, moving through the night.

The westward breeze had returned. Strengthened, in fact. And grown noticeably cooler.

Gritty dust rode the breeze, peppering his face and making him squint.

Then they were drawing close to the enclosure. Not wanting to get shot by Pipher or Gentry, Heck shouted, "It's us! We're coming back in!"

There was no shot from the sentries, only a triumphant whoop from Gentry.

Mabel Duncan stepped aside from the mouth of the passage and let them pass. She had her boy with her.

Now, what were they doing here? Where was Pipher?

Bruce stopped with his family while Heck rode into the enclosure, followed by Clarence and Cody, a passel of horses and mules, and the glorious spoils of war.

"You did it!" Becky cried. She ran to Cody and put her hand on his leg and looked up at him, talking rapidly.

Whatever she was saying was lost when the Count, who came stalking straight at Heck, shouted, "I told you we should have executed Pipher! He deserted—after robbing us blind!"

"He took our horses, our guns, our canteens, our food, everything," the Countess complained.

White hot anger lanced Heck's heart. Pipher had abandoned them when they needed him most. And he'd taken Red with him!

But he was careful not to show his anger. These folks needed a leader now, not more emotion.

"We're okay," Heck said. "We just did the same thing to the Sioux."

He pulled one of the extra rifles from the horse and handed it to the Count, who accepted it with a scowl.

"Better check that rifle," Heck said. "We gotta check all of them. We might need them any second now."

"I'll take one," Sergeant Gentry called from the bench. "I gave my rifle to Mrs. Duncan."

Heck went halfway up the rope ladder and handed the rifle to Gentry, along with some shot and powder, a canteen, and a fistful of biscuits. "Get back up top," Heck told him. "Eat and drink. I reckon we're in for it now."

Gentry nodded. "I'm ready for them."

"Good man," Heck said. He moved around the enclosure, distributing weapons, food, and water, while Cody and Becky led the animals back to the nearly dry pools.

As Heck worked, the Count followed him, demanding they go catch Pipher and get their things back.

"No way, Count," Heck said. "We ride out there now, we'll die."

"I am not a coward, Mr. Martin," the Count declared. "Who will ride with me?"

"Those Injuns are all stirred up," Cody said, coming back to them with Becky at his side. Heck was glad to see she held a rifle, too. "Heck's right. We go out there now, we'll die."

"Cowards!" the Count shouted.

Heck didn't have time for another one of the Russian's threat-laced tantrums. "You want to go, go."

"All right, I will! Natalia, fetch me a horse. The best one. And speaking of the best," he said, pointing to the other rifle sitting in Heck's scabbard, "give me that Enfield. It is mine."

Heck shook his head. "It was yours, once upon a time, but the Indians took it from you. And then I took it from them. It's mine now."

Truth be told, Heck didn't care about the rifle. He was just sick of the Count trying to bully everyone. And besides, why give it back to the Indians? He'd meant what he'd said about the Count's idea being suicidal.

"So you are a thief, too, eh?" the Count said. "I should have known. You Americans have no class, no character. Natalia, hurry up with that horse!"

"Leave it," Heck called to the Countess. "You folks want to

chase Pipher, you can do it on foot. Those horses don't belong to you, and I'm not giving them back to the Sioux."

The Count's eyes flashed with rage, and he spewed a stream of angry Russian. He started to bring the rifle barrel around but stopped when Heck swung his own barrel first, pointing it straight at the Count's chest.

"I don't appreciate people pointing weapons at me," Heck told him. "I let you go last time you did it, but let me be clear. If you point a weapon at me again, I will assume you intend to kill me, and I will react accordingly. There won't be a warning. You'll just be dead. Understood?"

The Count stared at him, red-faced with anger. He turned on his heel and marched off toward the enclosure.

"Keep an eye on him," Heck told Cody. "If the Count tries to ride out of here, shoot him."

"Gladly," Cody said.

"All right, everybody," Heck said. "What we need to do is—"

There was a pounding of hooves outside.

"Riders coming!" Bruce Duncan shouted from the front.

Heck and the others rushed forward.

"Not riders," Mabel Duncan said. "Just horses."

And there was Red.

The big stallion came prancing into the enclosure, snorting and looking for Heck, who came forward to welcome his oldest friend.

Following Red were all the other horses that Pipher had taken.

But where was the deserter?

Heck didn't care. He smoothed a hand over his old friend's neck, overjoyed to be reunited.

"My gems!" the Count said, charging out from cover. "Where are my gems?"

"I don't see them," Heck said.

The Count circled Red, searching him frantically. "No, it can't be true. Where is the box? Where are the gems?"

The breeze strengthened, cooling the air and bringing with it a sharp unmistakable smell that surprised Heck.

A distant booming sounded to the west.

"Army's coming," Sergeant Gentry called down from his watch. "I hear cannons."

"That isn't cannon fire," Heck called back. "It's thunder."

Wind whistled across the enclosure, whipping their clothing, and rushing away erratically, the way wind does when it's running ahead of a massive storm.

Far to the west, a massive, mightily forked lightning strike fractured the darkness.

There was a storm coming. A huge storm, as befitted the death of a long and blistering drought.

It would bring rain, of course, rain and wind, and it would hammer this open ground with bolts of sizzling electricity.

"It's fixing to rain," Cody called from the pools. "The wells are gonna fill back up. We can hold out here for a long time."

"And the Sioux know that," Heck told him. "They can't wait anymore. They will either ride out of here or come for us... now."

The wind blew stronger, bearing an eerie sound, a high-pitched scream that stretched on and on and on, then guttered low, becoming a deep bellow, the words of which were thankfully lost in the wind.

"What is that?" Becky asked with a shudder.

"Pipher," Heck said. "They captured Pipher."

"What's that horrible sound he's making?"

"They're torturing him."

CHAPTER 46

P ipher was still gibbering when the storm arrived, slamming into Petit Wells in a fury of roaring wind, pounding rain, and a barrage of hail that snapped down out of the angry sky like shotgun pellets.

The lightning was fearsome. Thunder shook the ground.

The Duncans replaced Sergeant Gentry in the hollow atop the boulders.

Cody suggested Becky join them up there, but she refused to leave his side.

They, Heck, and the others sheltered under the rimrock and lay with their rifles just inside the curtain of pouring rain. Staring through that curtain was like lying behind a waterfall and trying to look out through it… into darkness.

Gusting wind roared inside the enclosure, making them squint as it drove rain sideways into their faces.

Lightning pounded out of the sky, striking just beyond the

enclosure. For an instant, the space within the boulders lit up noonday bright then sliced away into darkness again.

There had been movement beyond the veil of cascading water.

As thunder shook the world, Heck realized what he had seen out there in the enclosure.

Horses.

Several of them, coming this way.

Clarence had seen them, too. "Riders coming," he announced, and someone fired.

Someone else followed suit. Then another rifle barked.

But Heck held his fire. Only a fool fires when he can't see his target.

Through the pouring rain, he saw the horses break and run, frightened by the gunfire.

Behind them came the real attackers, several Sioux warriors charging on foot through the rain, having used their horses as cover.

Their rifles stabbed flame as they reached the enclosure.

Someone to Heck's right cried out.

Heck and a few others returned fire.

Then the shadowy figures raced out of the sheeting rain and into the dark space where Heck and the others scrambled up to meet them.

One of the warriors slammed awkwardly into Heck, who staggered backwards and fired his Colt.

But then everything was a confusion of bodies fighting in the dark, and Heck no longer dared to shoot.

He rushed forward, seized a figure by the shoulders, and

tossed him aside, not certain if the person had been friend or foe.

A rifle butt slammed into his ribs, knocking the wind from him.

Heck lashed out with his revolver, striking with the barrel, and someone fell to the ground.

He waded forward, punching.

A knife slashed his arm.

His knuckles crashed into the back of a silhouette, and in the wild, flickering light of a lightning strike, he saw that man to be a Sioux warrior plunging a knife into the Countess.

Heck prodded the man with his muzzle and pulled the trigger, and the invader fell to the ground.

Someone behind Heck fired, and he staggered with the concussive blow of the sound and hissed with pain as he felt the bullet shear away part of his ear.

Others were firing now, too.

Heck heard the telltale whump of rounds hitting bodies. Ricochets whined all around.

Above, gunshots erupted atop the enclosure. As Heck had expected, warriors were coming over the walls.

For a few wild seconds, everything was gunfire and screaming, slashing and stabbing, bodies coming together and falling away.

Heck's hip jerked back so forcefully it twisted him halfway around and knocked him to the ground. At the same time, a boot crashed down on his hand, and he lost the Colt.

That was all right.

In this chaotic moment, with everyone fighting at close

quarters in complete darkness, a bullet was as likely to kill a friend as an enemy.

Likewise, he couldn't risk striking with his Bowie or tomahawk.

He staggered to his feet, hip throbbing.

He knew he'd been shot but didn't let it stop him, and he surged back in, punching and shoving, elbowing and kneeing, driving forward and smashing his way through everyone in his path.

A blade burned across his chest, but he didn't slow his wild attack.

This was no careful boxing match where he might hang back and pick his shots. Heck slid into a berserk rage, smashing through the ranks, punching and shoving, grabbing and throwing, incapacitating everyone in front of him.

How long it lasted, Heck couldn't have said. He was in a place outside of time, a place where he swung and smashed, bellowing like a wild beast as he pounded his way through anyone still standing.

And then, suddenly, it was over.

One of the Sioux gave the command, and the remaining warriors retreated as one, fleeing the battle.

In the flash of lightning, Heck saw the last of them disappear out of the passage.

"Get to cover!" Heck told his friends. He was breathing hard and hurting all over. "And reload. They might fire from the passage."

But his concerns came to nothing. There were no additional gunshots.

And then the storm, too, whipped away, as if chasing after the warriors.

CHAPTER 47

Clarence got a fire burning, and by its flickering illumination, Heck surveyed the aftermath.

Becky lay upon the ground, her face hidden behind a veil of golden curls.

Cody crouched beside her. His shirt was a bloody mess, and one of his eyes was swollen completely shut. He gently brushed the hair from her face.

Clarence pointed his rifle at the passage. He looked composed enough, but he had a livid slash across one cheek, and there was something wrong with his rifle.

The butt of the stock had broken away.

Likely snapped it off clubbing folks at close quarters, Heck thought and wondered briefly, remembering the blow of a rifle butt, if one of those people had been him.

It didn't matter. They had all fought bravely and blindly, which had been the only way to survive.

And survive they had.

Or at least, most of them had.

Heck studied the others and searched out his revolver, which still had four rounds in it.

The Count leaned over the Countess, who was clearly dead.

Sergeant Gentry had been killed too, dying with his rifle in his hands.

Four Sioux lay dead upon the ground.

Heck shook his head. So much destruction. So many pointless deaths.

He opened the Colt's cylinder and blew out the barrel to clear any dirt then snapped it shut again.

With Cody's help, Becky sat up, muttering. One cheek was swollen and already dark with bruising.

Heck's heart hammered, and the pain worsened, wounds everywhere announcing themselves as his battle rage ebbed away. He could hear his heartbeat in his right ear, the one that had lost part of its lobe.

Reaching up, he discovered the upper tip was gone.

He'd been shot and stabbed, bludgeoned and punched, kicked and bitten. Wounds ached all over his body, front to back, head to toe.

He knew he was bleeding but didn't know how bad.

He would check himself later. His body was fully functional for now. That's what mattered.

Because he needed to make sure the Indians weren't going to come charging back.

With aching hands, he reloaded the Colt's empty chambers, then fashioned a torch and went to check the passage.

The warriors were gone.

They had ridden off, leaving blood trails and the hoofprints of a few horses in their wake, disappearing into the first light of morning as dawn glowed faintly to the east.

They had done it. They had repelled the invaders. They had survived.

Heck called back to the others, telling them the Sioux had ridden off, and folks staggered forward.

The Duncans emerged from their elevated post. Both Bruce and Mabel had been injured, but neither was wounded grievously, and young Simon had escaped without so much as a scratch.

They had killed one warrior and wounded others, catching them as they climbed onto the wall.

Heck thanked God that things had gone so well. Yes, they had lost folks, and most of them were wounded, some severely, but things could have gone much, much worse.

It was over. It was all over.

Off to the northeast, a final lightning bolt split the sky.

As its thunder died away, a voice behind Heck called, "Martin!"

He turned, and there, fifty feet away, was the Count, who had apparently recovered his revolver, because there it was in his hand, pointing, despite Heck's clear warning, straight at Heck's heart.

Heck's Colt was in his hand, but it was below his waist, pointing at the ground.

"I had hoped the Indians would kill you and save me the trouble," the Count said.

"Why bother killing me?" Heck said, slowly angling the barrel of the Colt upward.

"Because you'll ruin my reputation, of course," the Count

said. "You'll spread my name across the West, telling lies about me."

"No need to tell lies," Heck said, bringing the Colt almost level. "The truth will ruin you."

Behind the Count, Heck's friends pointed their weapons.

"Put down the gun," Cody told the Count.

But this time, the Count paid no attention to Heck's friends.

And Heck said, "It's all right, boys. I already told him what would happen if he pointed his gun at me again."

The Count shouted with exasperation, and Heck threw his upper body to the left, leaning hard as the Count fired and missed.

Heck punched his own weapon forward and pulled the trigger.

Struck by Heck's bullet, the Count staggered backward and fired again.

Heck felt the shock of the bullet as it slammed into his chest, felt himself falling to the ground—but not before firing his Colt once more.

Fifty feet away, the Count toppled face-first into the ground, never to move again.

CHAPTER 48

I t was midday, three days after the big fight.

The storm had broken the drought and ushered in weather that was nothing short of delightful.

The wells were full again.

From the Indian camp, they recovered plenty of food along with grain for the horses.

They had also recovered the Count's lockbox, not in the Indian camp but close to the remains of Hank Pipher, who had clearly died a most terrible death.

They parceled out the gems and jewelry evenly or as evenly as they could, not knowing the various items' values. One thing was for certain: they all had enough to rebuild their lives.

For Cody and Becky, that life would be shared. They intended to head back East to her family, get married, and buy a farm.

The Duncans, too, would be backtracking at least as far as Hope City, where they planned to settle.

Clarence didn't know what he would do.

But yes, everything was going incredibly well.

Except, of course, Heck Martin was dying.

The big man lay beside the pools, delirious with fever, calling out for his wife and children.

Clarence had stayed by his side for three days, telling Heck to hang on, telling him everything was going to be okay.

But as time dragged on, Clarence saw that he was wrong.

He'd seen people hurt bad before, but not like this, not like Heck.

The man was tough as nails. That was for sure. But he'd taken too much damage.

Worst of all was the chest wound the Count had afflicted, but Heck might have pulled through if that had been the only injury. As it was, his body couldn't fight all the wounds at once.

He was burning up now, growing less coherent, and a troubling rattle had invaded his breathing.

It was hard to watch such a good, strong, brave man die, but a team of mules couldn't have dragged Clarence away. He would stay by Heck's side no matter how bad it got, no matter how long it took.

But then something happened that forced Clarence away.

"Riders coming!" Cody called from the northern wall. "There's a whole bunch of them!"

Clarence rushed forward, rifle at the ready.

They had known it might come to this, known the Sioux might come back with reinforcements.

"Are they Indians?" Mabel Duncan asked, putting voice to Clarence's concern.

"No, ma'am," Cody said, and smiled down at them. "No, ma'am, they're not."

As it turned out, however, the first rider through the passage was an Indian. Or part Indian, anyway. He was a fierce-looking young man who asked for Heck as soon as Cody hailed him.

Riding into the enclosure, the young man, who introduced himself as Seeker Yates, leapt from his horse and rushed to Heck.

A moment later, newcomers flooded the enclosure. There were fifty or sixty of them, all ready for war, and Clarence quickly learned they had ridden from Hope City, ready to charge Hades with a bucket of water if their friend Heck Martin was in trouble.

Sadly, it was too late for Heck.

Clarence told them as much.

"Shoot," Seeker said with a disdainful look. "My big brother ain't gonna die. He don't know how to die. He's too darn tough."

"Let me take a look," said a broad-shouldered, bespectacled man carrying a black satchel. He crouched beside Heck and started examining him with great focus.

"You're gonna be all right, big brother," Seeker said. "Doc'll patch you up."

The bespectacled man spoke to those who'd ridden with him. "Well, folks, better settle in. We're going to have to stay here for a while. Heck won't be well enough to travel for several days."

"Can you save him?" Becky asked, strangled with tears. "Will he really live?"

The doctor blinked at her with a look approaching confusion. "Of course he'll live, ma'am. He's Heck Martin."

———

A WEEK LATER, WHEN HECK WAS FINALLY READY TO TRAVEL, THEY all set out for Hope City together.

Clarence was incredibly relieved.

Heck Martin was the finest person he'd ever met. The world would be a far better place with him in it.

These others were good folks, too, and Clarence had decided he would give Hope City a try after all.

For fourteen years, he'd been running from the past. Now, at last, he was riding toward the future.

Beside him, the boy named Paul lifted his rifle.

They were riding past the burnt wagon and the Indian camp, where a lone buzzard hunched among the corpses, doing what God created buzzards to do.

"Leave him," Clarence said, pushing the boy's barrel aside before he could kill the bird.

The boy gave him a confused look.

"Me and that buzzard have history," Clarence said. "Let's just say I owe him one."

And on they rode, leaving the buzzard to his life and plodding forward into their own.

EPILOGUE

S ummer, 1871

"WHAT DO YOU SAY, OLD FRIEND?" HECK ASKED, FEEDING RED A piece of the apple he'd quartered for him.

Red, now closing in on thirty, had slowed down some over the years, but he was still big and strong and not so old in some ways, as was evidenced by all the reddish coats among this year's foals in Heck's Valley.

At thirty-seven, Heck himself was in the prime of life. Oh, he had some aches and pains, and whenever it rained, some of his old wounds pained him, but he was stronger than ever and, thanks to a life packed with reading and experiences, wiser as well.

The most important lessons life had taught him were simple: work hard, love your family, and count your blessings.

A man can build a good life sticking to those three things. A very good and surprisingly full life.

Every day, Heck thanked God for his family, friends, and situation.

Hope City had grown quite a bit and was now growing faster than ever, thanks to the Transcontinental Railroad, which had been completed two years earlier and in which Heck had invested heavily.

Beneath Heck's financial blessings, even his survival was miraculous, given all the scrapes he'd seen.

Like the time he'd been shot in the back after fighting a grizzly.

Or that time down in Petit Wells, thirteen years earlier, when Seeker and Doc had shown up just in time to save him from enough wounds, parceled out, to kill half a dozen men.

Or the numerous times he'd evaded death during his four years alongside Seeker in the Civil War, fighting to preserve the Union.

But he was thankful for a lot more than mere survival.

If someone had told him twenty-three years earlier, when Heck was a fourteen-year-old orphan heading west from Kentucky, that he would one day be an incredibly wealthy father of twelve happy children, he wouldn't have even believed it; but God had blessed Heck and Hope over the years, giving them eight healthy sons and four healthy daughters.

And soon, they would likely be grandparents, since their oldest daughter, Faith, had just married Tor's best friend, Simon Duncan.

Tor himself remained a bachelor, much to the chagrin of many young ladies in Heck's Valley.

But something burned in Tor, a restless yearning that Heck understood all too well.

At nineteen, Tor was six feet three inches tall with broader shoulders and bigger muscles than his father. The boy had mastered everything Heck had taught him: fighting and shooting, riding horses and working cattle, hunting and fishing and staying calm when others lost their heads.

Tor had read all of Heck's books multiple times and always impressed his father during their long, daily talks.

In many ways, Tor was an old soul and certainly quite wise for his years, but that youthful restlessness remained.

And now the boy had left them.

This very morning, in fact.

With the blessings of Heck, Hope, and his Uncle Seeker, who had done a lot of rambling himself in the years since the war, Tor had set off to travel the West.

Heck was happy for him. Excited, even. And, of course, a little anxious. Because Heck knew all too well the many dangers of the trail.

Heck already missed his son as he might miss his own heart.

"Please watch over my boy, Lord," Heck prayed aloud, "and please help him to become the man You would have him be. In Jesus' name, amen."

Then, turning toward the north, he saw a sight that filled him with joy.

Because here came Hope, riding toward him with a smile on her lovely face.

And she really was lovely. In fact, at thirty-seven, Hope was more beautiful than ever before. Her long, auburn hair flowed behind her, and her bright smile and emerald eyes shined with health and happiness.

Yonder is my wife, Heck thought. *The first and foremost blessing. The blessing upon which all other blessings have been built.*

"You asked to see me, Mr. Martin?" Hope said, reaching him, and he could see that her eyes were still red and puffy from Tor's departure.

"I did," he said, helping her down and pulling her into an embrace. "How are you holding up, my love?"

"Not bad, considering my boy rode off today. Do you really think he'll be all right, Heck?"

"I do. He's a smart young man and very capable."

"He's his father's son through and through."

"He's more than that. He's his mother's son, too. He'll be just fine."

She gave him a squeeze, broke their embrace, and smiled up at him. "You always make me feel better, Heck."

"And you always make me feel better, Hope." He glanced up the wooded hillside across the river. "Special day today."

"That's one way to put it. Though I have to say it's more sad than special to me."

"Well, there's something else that makes today special."

She cocked her head a little. "Now, what is that?"

"You don't know?"

She smirked up at him. "If I knew, I wouldn't ask, sir. Are you going to tell me or not?"

"Why tell you when I can show you instead?"

He led the way down the path. They followed the river then climbed the old trail up to the ridge, chatting about the children and Hope's parents, who were both doing well but completely devastated by Tor's departure.

The boy left a hole, that was for sure.

Heck took her all the way up to the rocky peak through the boulders to the edge of the big hayfield, which glowed in the mellow light of the afternoon sun.

They had recently cut the hay. Birds swooped joyously over the stubble, snatching bugs out of midair.

"Well, do you remember now?" Heck asked.

"Remember what?"

"Why today's so special?"

"No," she said. "I've had a hard day, Heck. Why don't you just tell me?"

He put an arm around her shoulders and pulled her close, and they stood together, looking out at the field.

"Let's just stand here for a minute," Heck said. "It'll come to you."

A moment later, Hope swiveled beneath his arm and stared into his face. "Is today June 18th?"

Heck laughed. "Yes, ma'am, it is. Twenty years ago today, we climbed up here together, and I asked you to marry me."

Suddenly, Hope was crying again. Only this time, they were tears of joy.

He held her.

"Oh, Heck," she said, "I'm so glad you asked me."

"And I'm so glad you said yes, Hope."

"God has blessed us beyond measure."

"Yes, He has."

"We've had a wonderful life, Mr. Martin."

"Yes, we have, Mrs. Martin, but we're just getting started, and I can't wait for every last day spent with you."

#

THANK YOU FOR READING *HECK'S STAND*.

I had a lot of fun writing this series, and I hope you enjoyed spending time with Heck and Hope.

Next up is *Lobo*, the story of a gunslinger raised by wolves. When seven men kill the priest who saved him from the wilderness, Lobo vows to hunt them down, no matter who they are or where they've scattered. Along the way, he'll rescue a young orphan girl, uncover long-buried secrets, and maybe do something a surly loner like Lobo would have thought impossible... fall in love. You can see the cover, read the blurb, and order a copy HERE.

If you enjoyed *Heck's Stand*, please be a friend and leave a review. When you leave even a short review, you just bought my family dinner, because Amazon will show the book to more people. I sure would appreciate your help.

If you enjoyed the book but don't have time to review, please consider leaving a 5-star rating. It's quick and simple and helps a lot.

I love Westerns and hope to bring you 8 or 10 a year. To hear about new releases and special sales, join my reader list.

Once more, thanks for reading. I hope our paths cross again.

Until then, don't approach a bull from the front, a horse from the rear, or a fool from any direction.

John

ABOUT THE AUTHOR

I was born six months before man landed on the moon and lucky enough to grow up in the country, where my family lived largely off the land.

When I wasn't fishing, exploring the woods, or weeding the garden, I devoured comic books like *Two-Gun Kid* and *The Rawhide Kid* before moving on to the exciting adventure stories of Jack London and Louis L'Amour.

Our black-and-white TV only got three channels, though you could lose one and pick up another if you went outside and messed with the antenna. On its grainy screen, we watched *Gunsmoke*, *Bonanza*, and movies starring John Wayne and Clint Eastwood.

Now a husband and father, I love traveling the West and reading history and fiction alike. My favorite authors are Louis L'Amour, Elmore Leonard, C.J. Petit, and R.O. Lane.

As a writer, I hope to entertain you with fun stories of the old West. My good guys are good, my bad guys are bad, and you'll always find a touch of romance to sweeten the grit.

If you'd like to keep in touch, join my newsletter HERE.

ALSO BY JOHN DEACON

A Man Called Justice (Silent Justice #1)

Justice Returns (Silent Justice #2)

Final Justice (Silent Justice #3)

Justice Rides Again (Silent Justice #4)

Destitution

Heck's Journey (Heck & Hope #1)

Heck's Valley (Heck & Hope #2)

Heck's Gold (Heck & Hope #3)

Heck's Gamble (Heck & Hope #4)

Heck's Stand (Heck & Hope #5)

Lobo (The Lobo Trilogy #1)